A

WO

Poems

—

Rhyming Short Stories

—

Short Stories without Rhyme or Reason

—

by Bernard W Roberts

—

Published by
NINA GIOTTI
Odyssey Works
Corporation Road
Birkenhead CH41 1HY
tel: 0151 647 2123
fax: 0151 666 1472
a trading name of Rhino P.G. Co. LTD.

A WORKING-CLASS LAMENT was first published in 2001 by NINA GIOTTI, at
Odyssey Works, Corporation Road, Birkenhead, WIRRAL CH41 1HY.
tel: 0151 647 2123 / 0151 666 1369
fax: 0151 666 1472
web site: www.rhinodirect.co.uk

ISBN 0-9538911-1-9

Typeset by Jenny Royle, Birkenhead, Wirral
Printed by Alphagraphics, Leeds LS2 9HZ

This book is dedicated to:

Harry Bowden Smith
Brian Hill
Peter Holden
Sir Freddie Laker

Four good men

Cover picture by the author's father, 'Grandpa' Roberts (1983).

CONTENTS

POEMS

RHYMING SHORT STORIES

SHORT STORIES

POEMS

a working-class lament

GORE BROOK

"D'yer know," the young boy said,
Throwing bread on the clear water
Where the river stood still,
"Why they call this the river that bled?"

The old man, wheel-chair bound
In his strait-jacket years,
Watched the child turnaround
And the ducks on the calm
Waters beside the weir
Where life's reflections disappear.

"No, do you?" the old man lied.

"This is where warriors were killed,"
The ten year old replied,
Proud of the battles that raged
On the river bank where he played.
"More than a hundred died,"
The excited child cried.

The old man smiled and nodded;
He knew the gore that once flowed
Was from the tanyard on the brow
With its black stench and wane;
And that gave the Gore Brook its name.

Sixty years ago, another boy
Had squeezed the tannin sap
From the oak and chestnut bark
For the dye pits above the park.

But the new boy would never know
The smell of death that filled the leat.
"Am off now," the boy shouted,
Walking towards the terraced street.

Alone on the small green plot
By the river he once made red,
The old man heard echoes on the hill:
"More than a hundred died,"
The young boy cried.

But the Gore Brook was transient:
It left no epitaph or mark
Of the old man in the park.

JENNIFER JOHNSON

Jennifer Johnson keeps out of the rain
And sleeps on the toilet holding the chain.
Sister of Mercy, flower in her hair,
Stooped clerks and shoppers stop, stand and stare
At the old woman with beer can in hand
With nowhere to go but who shuffles and
Whispers from Pierhead to Southdocks and down
By the Dingle and then back towards town,
Passed the Cathedral off Parliament Street,
Paint-peeling ceilings and dirty concrete,
Dust-covered windows and damp rotting rooms,
Girls on street corners, cheap smelling perfume,
Spiked railings and schoolboys who whistle and jeer
At Jennifer Johnson drinking her beer;
Catching the drips from her chin as she swears;
Cursing the schoolboys for nobody cares
For the old woman in ill-fitting clothes –
But where does she come from? Nobody knows...

EMPTY HOUSE

It was the council that cleared
The smell of death and decay
From the dark corner cupboard
Where the child had left its dust
Sixty years ago at play.
And brown-flowered paper peeled
From the walls like eighty-ply rust.

Built in 1864
Of black brick and Welsh grey slate
To house the industrial poor,
With flagged floor and iron grate,
The soot-stained two-up and down
Stood free of humanity
As it had four times before.

But there, once lived a new bride
Firm of breast, buttock and wrist
Who would donkey-stone the step
And at sink and bed perspire
To fulfil her wifely role.
In time she became a sage
And her neighbours bared their soul.

When her husband died, the house
Fell into damp disrepair
With old fermenting odours
And like shadows in the night
She began to transmutate
To that stranger on the street...

Then they came to fumigate.

THE ENTERTAINER

Alone, like a lost child grown old
On nicotine and acid rain,
The grey man stood on the corner,
A street-dancer without a name.

Humble at the factory gate
Where the black walls were ten feet tall
And sealed-in the machines and men,
Until the midday's siren call.

In overalls and on the move
The oily crowd poured on the street
And the old man with upturned cap
Played a tune with his dancing feet.

Like a puppet in wooden shoes,
A wrinkled face and rheumy eyes,
For the half-pennies on the ground
He stamped his clogs in double time.

In hollow cheeks he sucked his gums
And tap, tap, tapped a tune on stone;
A shuttle on a concrete loom;
Every Friday afternoon.

The stone's still pitted where he tapped
But otherwise you wouldn't know
An old man danced outside a gate
And crumbling walls of Jericho.

ONCE UPON A TIME

Once upon a time a factory
At the top of our terraced street
Made elaborate chamber-pots
With roses and forget-me-nots
For the American antique trade
All proudly labelled: 'British Made'.

Behind the gas works and Co-op
Real multi-coloured trains were built
With sweat and blood and ferrous steels
And massive calibrated wheels
That travelled the world and conveyed
Their brass-plaqued message: 'British Made'.

Up the road from the loco sheds
Like a black lobster on the hill
William Arkwright's four-story mill
Shuttled shuttles throughout the night
Weaving cloth for dye work tanks
With the appendage: 'Made in Lancs'.

The weekend work and double time
Brought Rock 'N' Roll in fifty-nine
And tattooed arms and bitter beer
And little extras for the wife
Like stilettos and fishnet tights.
They thought they all had jobs for life.

The Loco was the first to close,
It locked its gates in sixty-nine,
And when Arkwright turned off the heat
The bulldozers rolled down our street
And uprooted the railway line
With its 'Made in Great Britain' sign.

Between green hills and Burger King
Where once a thousand workers toiled
To keep the export market oiled,
A cash-and-carry super store
Sells plastic goods in paper bags
Attached to 'Made in China' tags.

GERIATRIC

She sits on the edge of the chair
In a cold ward of eight lost souls
Now geriatric grey and bent,
A woollen blanket heaven sent.

But beneath the arthritic pain
In features from antiquity
There's an elegance that remains
With gestures of feminity.

Like a flower sucked dry of life
Its seeds well scattered on the wind
Alone she stares back into time
At untold stories in her mind.

But the woman refined of face
In winceyette and fluffy shoes
Prays everynight to God to die –
For her, it's living that's the lie.

DANCING WITH FRED ASTAIRE

Blonde and willow slim, an inviting smile,
She was belle of the ball in '46
With Evening in Paris behind her ear,
A cigarette holder and painted lips.

In their Palais-de-Dancing patent shoes
The romeos in starched striped collars queued
And over-excused the 'excuse me' dance
While her sequins shimmered to drum and sax.

She listened to the whispered mating calls
From the brilliantine-smooth men of war
But she'd left her thoughts in the front seat stalls;
And vowed love for all but loved none at all.

Living with mam and dad in '59
She did piece-work and overtime and watched
The Black and White Minstrels on the tele
And on Sundays went to church with Nelly.

In the late sixties the factory closed
And the corner shops were falling down.
Unemployed and family in decline
A black couple moved into number nine.

In the summer of '77
With posters and saris she'd never seen,
Bombay and Karachi moved into town
And like her love-letters the street turned brown.

In '88 and feeling out of place
With greying hair, thin lips and ashen face,
Her new neighbours talked with inflections rare.
And her only white neighbour said 'don't stare' .

In '99 in an old-person's flat
On the first floor with pillows for support
She sat alone and sprayed for daily breath
And muttered to herself of this and that.

But now and again on Radio Two
She heard the strings of Rhapsody in Blue,
And in a satin dress and flowered hair
She was dancing again with Fred Astaire.

THE HAND

It was the eve of another birthday
And I watched the soft hand moving the pen
As it searched for a word to rhyme with time
The way a blind man walks behind his stick.
There were more brown spots than I could recall
When they marked my growing pains on the wall.

My father was not a scholarly man,
His talents were on the factory floor
But his brush-strokes could make swans skate on snow
And crippled beggars waltz the Barcarolle.
Fine art compared to my acerbic rod
That fly-fishes syllables from the soul.

But no captured words or imagery
Could recreate my black and white picture
Of him standing suited against the sun
Like a businessman with bandaged hand,
In cycle-clips and triangular sling;
A day off work for losing half-a-thumb.

The years of wrestling with quarter-inch thick
Wire in Galvani's molten bath that writhed
Like steaming snakes could not intimidate
The shapes he sculpted from sulphurous lead,
While the slimmer hand of his eldest son
Fought nothing more than the commercial pen.

He was a man proud of his old flat cap,
Ragged overalls, barbed wounds and broken bones.
No self-praise or fancy intonations
From the artisan with the gravel hands
That held mine when I sat on his shoulders
And led me to the cherry blossom lands.

I listened to the wood pigeons cooing
Above lawn-mower men and wigged women
In cultivated teeth and venetian
Blinds where neighbours watch four bedroomed detached,
And the middle-aged and middle-classed
Wear their designer labels on their hats.

There were only two stanzas to write but
It was growing dark and I fell asleep
To dream of inefficient lawyers,
Accountants' fees and Value Added Tax,
Of high bank charges and low sales returns,
The minimum wage on the camel's back.

When I awoke on my sixty-second
I saw my father in the looking-glass,
And the black priest and burial balm.
But the tired face faded behind the steam.
He had appeared older than yesterday,
As did the softer hands he had bequeathed.

SATURDAY NIGHT

There was a gold sheen where the brush had been
More than a hundred times that afternoon,
And feeling all grown-up and debonair
She tied a yellow ribbon in her hair.

On the three-mile ride down a dusty road,
She sat like a queen on the bus to town
Thinking of nothing but her new-found friend
With a proper job and money to spend.

It was that time of day when peace descends
And she walked down the street in creaking shoes,
But, as before a storm, the air was still
While a pigeon watched from a window sill.

The mid-summer evening was humid
With gossamer clouds suspended beneath
A sky splashed like shot-silk in cream and blue,
And shyly she walked past the theatre queue.

On the street corner away from the crowd
The overheated blood raced through the veins
Of the tidy young schoolgirl who waited
For blue-eyed Bill, the boy she had dated.

When the neons lit up the breathless town,
They painted moving shadows on the ground
Where wide-eyed youths walked in future tense
And talked in a language that made no sense.

The nearby beerhouse gasped through open doors
Where undernourished and black-suited men
Leaned on beer-stained counters in the half light,
Laughing at the girl alone in the night.

For an hour on the doorstep she waited
For the very first boy she had dated;
But the subject of mirth and down-hearted,
She crept back up the street and departed.

CONFLICT

Conflict, you are my constant companion.
Go away, let me be. I need to rest
from your daily visits and opinion
in the never-ending human contest.

Discourse is like morphine to an addict,
stirring the flames of the commercial fire.
Anxious to disagree and contradict
is the condition to which you aspire.

Yes, Conflict, you, the purveyor of rage
and all those other four letter words that
you release from those who normally cage
the expletives that you are expert at

formulating and hurling like barbed-wire
until all logic is lost in hellfire.

RESURRECTION

At night when your eyes look inside
The concavities of the skull
Exposing shadows that reach out
Like bent grave-diggers in the mist
Who dig up the forgotten dead
And bury sanity instead.

At night when the flesh feels no pain
But there's a movement in the womb
You try to sleep but dream alone
And search the corners of the room
Where creatures you cannot recall
Appear like patterns on the wall.

At night when the devil visits
To stoke and stir you in your bed
And when the maidenheads undress
To run the gauntlet of the flesh
And dance macabre inside your head,
Remember, you exhumed the dead.

THE WEB

She wove a web and the thread
Was the work of all her days.
It was from the outer edge
That I looked in with regret
And other mixed emotions
At the scant regard she'd paid
To aspects of a journey
That had manufactured pain;
And concentrics of a life
That I thought was infinite.

The web's centre was a heart,
Inconsistent at the start
But defining with the years
Into a maturescent verse.
Then the decades plucked the strings
And the bow became a ring.
Like the circles of the mind
They were running out of time,
For the core had worn away
And a year became a day.

Like the birthdays of an oak
The years had passed by unseen
But the weaver wore a cloak
Like an ancient Homer queen.
Hand-sewn on Medusa's spindle
In snakeweed that fell apart
And hung like bits of tinsel
On a moulting Christmas tree.
A redefining work of art,
A web broken by decree.

---

20 LINES ON A LIFE

Sunlight slanted across the living-room.
It was midmorning and my mother stood
Cradling my baby sister to her chest.
Knee-high, I held on to her flowered dress.
" Hello, love," the woman from next door said,
Walking into the house, red faced and round,
And sucking her gums as though chewing bread.
" How long, love?" she asked, with a rasping sound.
She touched the infant's head and a tear fell
From my mother's cheek on the swaddling clothes;
And the women, two generations apart,
Faced each other in the warm morning sun
While my sister and I were in the dark.
" She looks lovely, love. It's hard to believe
She's dying. Are you sure that's what he said?"
My mother nodded. " Don't cry, mam," I begged.
The baby moved her head, looking at me.
" Oh God: she's dead," the old women exclaimed.
" No, she's looking at her brother," mam sighed.
But then the baby's head fell to the side.

THROUGH BARNIE BLOODHOUND'S BLOODSHOT EYE

Polluted river, detergent fed,
his lifeline runs from left to right;
suffers from the thoughts of death
and drinks old ale on Friday night.

Buxom brunette reads a mystery,
Barnie Bloodhound notwithstanding
twists a lilac in his hand,
crawls along decrepit landing.

Sneezing beneath an insipid moon,
licks his lips in the silhouette;
for her flesh sings hosanna;
amber foglight plays the piano.

Disorganized in combinations,
unfurls her stocking top to toe,
recollects in the mirror:
Mothers of Mercy come and go.

Dishonourable thoughts in his head,
Barnie Bloodhound in a turmoil:
obedient to his glands,
elevated at the parboil.

Avaricious with the facts of life,
repulsed he grinds and stabs false teeth;
unleashed anger fumes and roars,
but buxom brunette sleeps and snores.

TWO-BY-TWO

The dying night bequeathed the dawn
A thin grey mist that weatherworn
And ragged rolled across the sea
To where black waters lapped the quay.

And there, aching at bow and stern,
A ferryboat groaned on the swell,
Its rattling chains against the rail
As mournful as St.Nick's church bell.

Sea-salt and diesel licked the air,
And like old bones before first light
A gangway creaked and fell to earth,
And seagulls screeched and fought in flight.

Like shadows on a wooden hill,
The solemn commuters waited
But the man in the black peak cap
Watched the clock and aggravated

The motley mass en route to work
As rigid as the ferry's beams.
At eight o'clock they walked the plank
Dragging onboard their fading dreams.

In borrowed space they walked asleep
Where crinolines and spats once passed,
For like the buried dead they are
The regulated underclass.

Two-by-two and inside their heads,
The frigid girls in floral flocks
And razored clerks in wasp-striped socks
Climbed back into their still warm beds.

Oilskin wrapped on an outer deck
And turtlenecked against the rain,
A nomad of rope and anchor
Struggled to lift the gangway chain.

A shoreman peeled the bollard clean,
Throwing the hawser at the feet
Of the matelot with missing teeth
Who shuffled to the Mersey's beat.

With grating power, the turgid
Waters churned metamorphic white,
And the urban crew sailed towards
The two stone birds in static flight.

At the Liverpool landing stage
The human tide, like black beetles
Exposed to light, scurried away;
Conformists for another day.

AD CAPTANDUM VULGUS*

(The Industrial Revolutionaries)

Bone, bone, ragbone, ragbone, they groan
As the shovel and chapel spire
And ancient knockers-up conspire
To raise the sleepers from their beds
With cigarettes and coughing heads.

Between torn dreams and greasy tea
As silent as the workhouse flea
They traipse to work in discontent
At gothic mills where cog-wheels grind
The flesh and mind with overtime
That every Friday pays the rent.

As rancid as the margarine
That lubricates the time machine,
On Saturdays they stand in line
Outside the frugal corner shop
For fish and chips and servitude;
But the cyclical clock consumes
Their time and tide and attitude.

And like manure beneath the snow
The diggers play adagio,
And stand knee deep in death and dust;
In ad captandum vulgus trust.

---

*Ad captandum vulgus (L):
To please the rabble.

HIGH TIDE

It was a stormy New Year's eve on the
slippery half-mile long, four persons wide,
semicircular, coast-to-coast divide,
awash with an 8.6 metre tide.

Those promenading, hoop-skirted ladies
a hundred years before would not foresee
that one day a solitary soul would be
walking biblically across the sea.

Like small waves, a hundred common gulls sprawled
on the lee side of the seaweeded wall,
while on the open sea, black-backed gulls trawled
and foraged fearlessly beneath the squall.

The gale-force wind was ice-bound and strident
at more than twenty knots, but the distant
shore lights pulsated inside a verdant
mist that concealed yesterday's excrement,

force-fed to the coast by a sewer pipe
where maternity and offspring conspire
to feed the vulval sea, swollen and dire
like over-yeasted bread grows under fire.

Battered and trapped by his own negligence
in the sceptical sea of indifference
that absolves all human decadence,
he waded through the swirling effluence

and other debris like Irish Sea stew,
bulbous gutweed and condoms from the loo,
deflated and flushed with the residue
of discarded umbilical tissue.

' Beware of the offshore wind and wave-form,'
the dock notice read – but he thought the storm
would pass and the strip of blue would transform
the twin dangers of which the notice warned.

In the beginning, he walked through the seaweed,
but was confident that he could proceed,
despite the gale-force wind and turning sea
that was now bombarding the man-made quay.

At the half-way mark the waves were severe
but the crashing, waist-high waves at the rear
forced him forward with subjugated fear
of falling in the raging hydrosphere.

Moving slowly with his life in peril,
he listened to the oystercatchers' shrill
call as they pushed and jostled for the thrill;
so like the screams that made his world stand still

when the storm shrieked and day turned into night.
He slipped but initially kept upright,
cursing his own stupid lack of foresight
and the cold, thirty degrees fahrenheit.

Where the land conjoins the harbour wall, he
stumbled, crawling like a beached manatee,
and dragged himself clear of the raging sea
as it finally overwhelmed the quay.

He was reminded as he stood drying
that storms are overcome not by crying;
and that he would not have been soaked in brine
had he taken note of the warning sign.

END OF AN ERA

From its eyrie, the one-eyed clock
As gothic as a guillotine
Glared down on the rookery town
And the people in gaberdine.

' Don't be late,' the time-keeper cried,
' Or we will dock you half a day.'
At seven o'clock they punched their cards
And production was underway.

At cotton mills and down the mine
With molten lead to galvanise,
The welder, turner and millwright
With engineer worked through the night.

In tallow-grease and paraffin
With screwdrivers, saws and hammers
And blood-stained hands they rasped and gasped
And manipulated spanners.

On the turgid factory floor
The flywheels spun the pirouettes
And lubricated hearts and minds
With noxious fumes and cigarettes.

For a hundred and fifty years
They broke their backs but took the blame.
And then one day the unions came
With promises of wealth and fame.

But the Eastern sun was rising
And ploughs and rakes were cast away
As the trading tide was turning.
It seemed the West had had its day.

With the ring of the final bell
The factory gates were opened wide
And the workers, battered and bruised,
Were carried on the ebbing tide

To street corners with leisure time,
Decreasing jobs but increasing crime,
With opiates to ease the pain
And illustrate the wax and wane.

The circus came to town one day,
It stayed a while then went away.

TOGETHER ALONE

Crumpled from crumbling head
to toe,
the tramp fumbles, mumbles sleepily
on the edge of the flat green patch
while the flagged and cold cemented streets
Tick-tock-tick like the townhall clock.

And we sit together alone.

And on the keep-off lawn,
silk-smooth
pigeons, silver grey and overfed
contest the clerical bread and
sally with indignant stares at the
coughing heads on the dole again.

And we watch together alone.

Around the flat green patch
of town,
noise and chemicals demand the right
to choke arterial veins that
ache against perspective years ahead
until the still electric night.

And we walk together alone.

And the old man nods his whiskered head
on the hardwood bench,
his bed,
beneath memorials of war and
pictorials of black plate-glass,
and lies inside himself unmade sleep.

And we sleep together alone.

THE BUSINESSMAN

(1)

Like a prowling beast of prey,
The businessman spends his day.
Not content with what he's made,
Always pushing and afraid.
Worrying – don't ask him why:
Rich or poor he's sure to die.

1966
Author's occupation: student

THE BUSINESSMAN

(2)

Actually he spends his day
Trying to make money to pay
Those stealth taxes this Government
Invents like the 19%
Hike on the misnamed 'council' tax,
And other charges on the backs
Of employers, like NI tax
On all their full-time employees,
Motorcars, petrol; what they please.
For more detail of what I mean,
Please refer back to page 13.

2001
Author's occupation: company director

THE POET

Relaxed in ancient thoughts of men,
Pope, Blake, Byron, men of the pen,
On what they thought of life and death
But long since drawn their final breath.

How in their span of years gone by
They questioned and puzzled why.
Was their reasoning all in vain?
So much effort, so little gain.

BY COMMON CAUSE

In carbolic and D D T
Where gangrenous wounds were sewn,
I stood tip-toe on a body box
And heard the wounded groan.
A few men whispered in the dark
And a shadow prayed alone.

With pockets filled with fleas and lead
And ulcerated thirst
I surveyed the plain for the nearly dead
And saw a figure cursed:
A youth beside a fractured tree,
Half a leg above the knee.

His bitten fingers of mittened skin
Rested on empty steel
But down below it was winter's rage
That slipped the safety pin
And aimed the barrel in the night
With a button in its sight.

Invisibly the finger moved
Across the shattered soil;
Saw reflections from the frozen eyes
Stare at the late recoil.
It was by word they heard the sound
Of their loved one on the ground.

AFTER THE CELEBRATION

Another Christmas Day arrived
With mistletoe and merriment,
And like the wine and Father Time,
Friends and relatives came and went.

After one more drink for the road,
Steve and Jean were the last to leave
For their two hundred yard drive home.
' See you in the New Year,' said Steve.

The noise from the lane was muted
But I went out into the night
And came upon a tangled mass
Of broken bones and shattered glass.

Bent and rigid in steel and smoke,
A deconstructed statuette
With interwoven rod and rib
Like modern art in silhouette.

Surrounded by tinsel and foil,
Steve's eyes stared into space,
Translucent in the hunter's moon
With death embossed across his face.

With an arm in touch with exposed heart,
Jean lay inside their tomb of blood,
A future florid epitaph
Of churned-up asphalt, oil and mud.

TERRA INCOGNITO

In the caretaker town
The watery silence
Played the stone-bed, half-dead
Bottle-sucked alleys and
Withered fingers of time.

Only the pitter-pat
Of the rodent on the roam
Worried the hollow road
Where the homeward bound crept
Towards tomorrow's door.

Blindly they walked on to
The holy day and saw
The threaded flesh that bled.
But the burnished palate
And sewer-rat foraged

In the blistered oil of
Hot dog gnawed in the damp
Informality of
Wedded hands drifting through
The soot veiled, time-stained night.

And a patch-eyed cat sat
Beside itself and watched
The debauched and stumbling
Imperfections move
Their bones beneath the moon.

ADRIFT

Timidity is the mother of lies,
With a skill more cunning than maternal;
So do not misconstrue what metrifies
As sunshine rhyme. It may be nocturnal..

The coward is an expert in deceit
Who, when back-to-back, will lie to ensnare,
But face-to-face will direct booted feet
On shins of those who lay deception bare.

Staring and indignant, the liar swears
That black is white in total innocence,
And questions how anybody could dare
Lower themselves to such impertinence

As to disagree with what they profess
To be the whole truth. But proceed with care
For the liar is careful to impress
That disbelief will cause untold distress.

And who are those people who lie so well?
Look around, there is often a liar
To be found two metres from where you dwell:
Man, woman, child and fresh-faced supplier

Of goods or services, and repair men
Who can confuse the consumer with science,
Sharpening a dull tradesman's acumen
With an out-of-warranty appliance.

Larceny is inate in the human
Psyche – but it is a question of degree,
And would take the wisdom of Solomon
To know the trickster from the Pharisee.

By implication then, it's in the genes
Like going bald or cancer of the breast;
The transexual who is epicene
But suffered from severe pains in the chest

And died from his father's heart condition.
Unlike obesity and lack of love,
The liar's genetic disposition
Is hidden like a hand inside a glove.

There are no exceptions to this failing:
Doctor, lawyer and government mislead;
And the media are daily unveiling
Headlines like 'if ' and 'may be' that deceive.

All these examples are monetary
And driven by greed and financial gain.
The lies in the following commentary
Are of a different kind and contain

Samples of what's beneath the human skin
And playing with other flesh called sin; so
With deception of the heart we'll begin
But in three stanzas end this fake rondeau.

'I did nothing,' he said, blameless and pure.
'I would not,' she lied, again and again,
As truthful as Cassio to the Moor,
And fearful of vengeance, not examen.

What is at the root of all this deceit
When we're supposed to know what's wrong and right?
Perhaps the reason why some steal or cheat
Is because it's integral to a psyche

That overdoses on television,
Unemployment, estrogen or the pill.
And without religious supervision,
Life can be an anagram of devil.

DOWN TOWN

It is Friday midday and all seems well:
Dark suits, smoke, pickled-eggs – another day;
Repetitions of fifty years before
With Ada, white and deaf, behind the bar

Breathing the disinfected city dust.
'Two pints of mild, love.' Cig-ends on the floor.
The old woman cups an ear, creaks and leaks
Veiled perspiration as she steers the years.

Shoulder to shoulder in self-interest
Clerks and travellers in monotones talk
While middle-aged vulnerability
Watches itself cracked in the white tiled wall.

Through the window the winter sun deceives.

AWAKENING

Last night we laughed
Outside was black
It kept us warm
Now comes the dawn

FACE TO FACE

The kindest thing to all mankind:
The front's the front and back's behind.

THE DANCE HALL

The smell of sweat and the cheap perfume,
The emptiness of the crowded room.

... AND LITTLE GIRLS ARE MADE OF ...

It's in my mind,
                    she said,
Where the gland twitched the nerve
that time was on her side
of half the night that bred.

                    she said,
It's in my mind always,
Where the bone outstretched the dream
she felt her own hot touch
beneath him in the haze.

                    she said,
It's in my fingered hair
(she'll never be a nun)
and then, it's in my mind
before the clock strikes one.

                    she said,
My naked body feeds
and then the lover's fight
is in my head in bed,
undressed I feel away
the night.

AFTER THE TIDE

Beside a shallow channel left
By the ebbing tide, a figure,
Bent double and in silhouette,
Dug a trench in search of lugs, and
Built a wall, ten feet long, of sand.

A shelduck, sharp in black and white,
Ratcheted up from the sea stream,
Slow and low away from the man.
Its red-beaked mate followed quietly,
Flying to a nearby island.

At the cross-roads of sea and land,
Curlews waded in search of food,
And between the veiled sea and man
A thousand burrowing knots dug
For worms – but built no wall of sand.

LITTLE GIRLS

" I'm a model for Vogue, " one cried,
And twisted and brushed back her locks
For the man with the little black box,
While another pushed her aside.

" ' er a model? " a third replied.
" She's nowt but the Gretham Street lag
But to friends she's Beryl the bag! "
In friendship they jostled and vied.

" Of course it's me they wanna see, "
The first one smiled, turning her head.
" No, it's me, " the second girl said.
While the quiet one asked:

" What's the fee? "

INNOCENCE AND ILLUSION

The summer wind blew across the valley
And carried the playing children's laughter
Across green and undulating pasture
Where the drum-beating river's rockery
Guided the rushing waters to the sea.
And a lone skylark sang in mockery.

Beyond the field where rabbits and spring lambs
Jumped in their own youthful celebration,
A sombre forest of moss-clad steeples
Stood on the hill like a congregation
Where nothing stirred but the nocturnal breath
Of the local fox family sleeping
And blank-eyed owl and creeping beetle.

At dusk, the children were called to their homes,
And rabbits burrowed and white lambs suckled
Until night's curtain draped the fir tree domes.
There the owl and lean fox watched and waited
Until the ewe and lamb separated,
And with baa and bleating the chase began –
But the fearful flock ran and stood apart
As the fox bit deep into throat and heart.

When the lamb was stripped to bone and red fleece,
And stars painted patterns of confusion,
Counting sheep, the young children fell asleep
And dreamed of innocence and illusion.

INFECTION

Let me take you into the inner sanctum,
the black hole
of an unemployed life.
Let me take you into the tomb of poverty.

It is a blind, mindless journey.
It is a short journey,
shorter than you think.

It is a voyage of struggle,
a voyage of empty dreams.
It is a voyage of despair.

It is a voyage
no longer than your yesterday.

Can you feel the cold black fear
against you like a skin,
leading you,
chaining you,
dragging you down, down, down
between the church and clinking
sidings in their symbolic silhouette?

Can you taste it;
the dry teeth and bile tongue
reining you,
pulling you,
dragging you on, on, on
with the cold black mist inviting
you to join the jobless in the park?

Can you hear it,
scratching, calling you
to the unemployment shop?

Listen to the statistics
calling, calling, calling
with the Far East wind.

Touch the withered flesh,
rheumatic limbs, bent and gnawed
on the crumbling bone.
Breathe in the stragnant air
and listen, listen, listen...
they are calling to you from the grave.

Listen to their pleas.
Listen or else they will overrun,
and infect you like the plague.

FEASTING ON THE SACRAMENT

When he breathed his last
His house was pillaged by his own
Events concurrent like the past
But the pieta stood alone.

Like the picture box,
The elephants without consent
Had walked with time and mantle-clocks.
Who did these actions represent?

The inner wall gone!
Like the deceased it disappeared,
No picture of the wedding gown
That graced that space for sixty years.

Fifteen years before,
His wife's demise was reverent
But his death was the open door
For feasting on the sacrament.

Without covenant
But a magpie need to realise
Enrichment from a weekly rent.
A wrecker's plan unauthorised.

The sermon began
With fire and fury in the prayer,
A swan-song for a hardy man.
But burning incense fouled the air.

LAMENTATION

Dad's dead, I heard the voice on the phone say.
He thought he'd live forever and a day.
A misconception we shared, I replied,
His vivid image dancing in my mind.

Dead? The man who could talk for hours on Keynes.
Dead? Oxford! He who read for Phd.
Dead? All his mature learning come to that.
Dead? How will the pub fill the gap.

How's your mum? I asked after drinking air.
She's okay, she said. She's fine. Life goes on.
I heard the fingers running through her hair.
When? Yesterday was the abstract reply.

Twenty-eight years of friendship down the line
Since we first discussed the philosophies
Of McCarthy, Karl Marx and Socrates,
Church and western industrial decline.

And the humanitarian principles
Of time, place and space we occupied
In the nicotine and cataleptic bar
Of braless barmaids and coughing catarrh.

We talked of Shakespeare and Renaissance man
Surrounded by narrow conversations
Of prejudice and intimidation
And blasphemy, sex and segregation.

Dead? He who dressed for comfort not disguise
And was looked down upon by lesser eyes.
Those who would never have an intellect
To compare if they lived a thousand years.

Dead? The man whose history I had shared
Through the short seasons of a working life
Of tar-macadam madness and routine,
Of mortgage payments and God Save The Queen.

It was a grey day when the hearse passed by
On its quiet penultimate ride
Along the road to wife and cold fireside.
I knew it was he by the coffin size.

In the carpet slippers he often wore
He was taller than those scornful men,
But as he journeyed down the road
I felt remorse that all life comes to nought.

I wondered if they had dressed him for town
Or in a gown – for a glass-sided hearse?
He would not have been found dead in a skirt.
He'd prefer an old cardie and plaid shirt.

What was on his mind just before he died?
Was it economic analysis
Of the Keynsian social theory kind?
Or a pint of bitter beer by his side?

I had no hat to raise in respect,
Nothing tangible to express those years
Of shared aspirations and life's concerns,
The balancing between nurture and work.

Goodbye, old boy, was his favourite phrase.
In a whisper I recipricated:
Goodbye, old boy, until we meet again.
A meaningless cliché – but sincere praise.

PASTIMES

You know the fellow
Works at your place
We see him at the cemetery

She said

But I sat on the edge
While the man in the pub
Leaned over the table
Hunched in a cloud
And built a house of sticks

He was alone
With a cornered eye that
Sifted the syllables of his mind
And spoke about the things he knew
A little of...

As whispering shadows
crossed the misty valley
the children ran to dusk

Four minutes from the end
We left him
Half of bitter in his hand

He'd thought about his past aloud
Then swept his efforts to the dust

You know the fellow
Works at your place
We see him at the cemetery...

ON WAKING

Morning came
With it's fried bacon smell
And the holy warnings
Of Sunday's sullen bell.

At midnight
With firm resolve intact
She turned her head, refused
To contemplate the act.

But mana
Was equal to the task
And by deceit infused
Behind a moral mask.

She lay down
With voices in her head
That argued with the church
And cried out on the bed.

Until dawn
Had bled the night away
And contradiction crept
Unwanted into day.

SANDSTONE, VANDALS AND VERSE

Where neither unleashed wind nor weed
Could dispossess the gravid seed
That lodged inside the liquid room
And sucked the fluid from the groom.

In the uterus of that night
As viscous as the stalactite
When January showered the earth
With seminal and hallowed birth.

With April rain the salt tears flowed
Until the trusty school gate closed,
And like a mountain stream they fell
With cuts and grazes. Time will tell.

The home-bell rang, the chains undone,
A chapter closed – the spring had gone;
No more to add or take away,
Excited on the first of May.

With ribbons flowing from their hair,
In ankle socks and cotton frocks
And button shoes they danced the tune,
Rejoicing on the twelfth of June.

But in July they multiplied
And with addition sympathised
For what they'd known but left unsaid
While lying on the suckling bed.

Then autumn's silhouettes blew cold
And mirrors told of growing old;
They'd trod the boards and played their parts
In the recycling of their hearts.

But winter-ravaged like dead sheep,
In sepia thoughts they fell asleep
With engraved stone above the head
And sombre sonnets left unread.

GLYN CEIRIOG

In polished shoes and Sunday best
And regimental rows.
He in a hat and thermal vest,
She with her hair in bows.

He's six feet down below the ground,
She's four feet and a jot,
With feet to east they're westward bound,
Carnations in the pot.

Buried in lipstick and cologne
And rouge and wedding ring.
But his smooth chin now turned to bone
And windsor knot to string.

Her tongue now still as four a.m.,
She wore his ears to stone.
She was the pain of valley men,
Her verbal skills home-grown.

The birds have flown, they left their sign,
The vultures came and fed,
Now Ethel's on his rosehip wine
With Cyril in their bed.

For economy in twos or more
This dogless land of nod,
No headstones for those right of door !
How will they talk with God ?

Here amid dust and bones
And good Welsh name like Glyn and Jones,
Alone with tales to tell
Is 19th century Jane Morrell.

As silent as the church-step fly
They lie beneath the grass;
Until they greet the next to die
And that will surely pass.

So remember these words I say
And go to St. Ffradds everyday,
Then in Glyn Ceiriog when you're ill
You're more than welcome on the hill.

THE VISITOR

The memories of childhood
Blew through the sepia streets
And the man heard a voice call
From the green valley below
And the shallow stream sat still.
'Hey there, come on down, ' it called
From where the trees climbed the hill.

But he walked along the brow
Above where the children and grass
And his past moved in the breeze
While the park birds sang unseen.
'Hurry up, ' whispered the leaves
On trees where no trees had been.

For a moment he lingered
By the fields where he once played
With those sleepers on the bench
But young mothers half his age
Watched the old man with the cane.
'On yer way, ' a woman cried
To the man on memory lane.

From his past he walked away
And the child inside the man
For the first time saw decay.

THE WORKMAN

With the odours of another day
Stepped out of bed; roof-tops and decay,
Two cold feet and oilcloth on the floor,
Somebody knocking on Monday's door.

In bib-and-brace and corduroy cap,
Stood in the queue for the number two,
On an upper deck with silent tongues,
Cigarette smoke and fermenting lungs.

With holes in the soles of shoes and socks,
Fell in line at the clocking-in box,
And with a whistle from foreman Sam,
Like a metronome, the work began.

Twelve hours at a rotating machine,
Thirty minutes in the works' canteen,
A breathless bus in the creeping rain,
Obscenities on the window pane.

A weary key in the latch at eight,
Cockroaches and cinders in the grate,
Egg and aspirin with two rounds of bread,
Then counted bolts in a restless bed.

THE MONASTERY

Prologue

Bound by Victorian
Leg-irons of ancient
And scarred desks where others
Too had trembled before
A young woman in black –
Now gaunt and bent of back.
"Quiet," she screamed. Wide-eyed
And bigoted she slammed
Her willow rod against
The partly opened door.
"Don't let me hear you breathe!"
She cried, stamping the floor
To stir the dust and tears.
After a breathless pause
The old nun laid the cane
Across the table top
And with interlocked hands
Continued: "Now we pray."
And the forty children
With elbows on their desks
Began: ".. give us this day – "
"Close your eyes, you bad boy,"
The taut teacher shouted,
Bending a creaking knee
Before the five year old,
Terrified and weeping.
Outside in soft sandals,
Brown monks shuffled sockless
Past the room with the rod
Where perhaps they too had
First felt the wrath of God.

EPILOGUE

But I cast off the chains
That had anchored my roots
To industrial grime
And navy boiler-suits.

The seasons came and went
And in those missing years
Two generations died
Of cigarettes and beers.

Once a community
Of Anglo-Saxon pride;
Now only one old aunt
Held back the Asian tide.

In her OAP flat
We talked of years gone by:
Of bowlers and Whit-walks
And home-made apple-pie.

"I'll see you in two weeks,"
I said, outside her door
Where communal odours
Matched the brown walls and floor.

On my way out of town
I drove towards my past
Where, like the empty streets,
The sky was overcast.

Sixty years on, the monks
And nuns had gone away
But the church looked unchanged
In several shades of grey.

It didn't look decayed
As I'd heard the news tell,
But I walked through the door
Into an empty shell.

Where sparrows flew freely
And wallowed in the mud,
And broken bricks and stone
Lay where the pews once stood.

Like the stained-glass windows,
The pieta had gone
With the lead and fittings
And clergy's demijohn.

Within these walls at Mass
The crowd arrived roughshod,
Stout-hearted in liquor
To show their faith in God.

Where in early April
Excited bride and groom
Queued and were sanctified
With a Catholic womb.

I thought I was alone
Until a tapping came
From behind a slab stone
Where a youth carved his name.

"What are you doing?" I said,
Seeing vandalism at work,
And inside a church at that!
He blew away the dirt.

"What's it ter yer?" he replied.
"This was a place for prayer,"
I fumed, but felt foolish -
Defending disrepair.

"This is a monastery,"
I yelled. "A place of God."
The skinhead turned and said:
"I couldn't give a sod."

"Doesn't your school teach you
About the Holy Ghost,
Matthew, Mark, Luke and John,
The Virgin Mary, son?"

"I don't know nowt about
Ghosts and that Matthew gang;
And the virgins I know
Are bleedin ' second ' and."

Staring into my eyes,
He bared his yellow teeth
While his blade continued
To probe the altar-piece.

"Christ," he said, and I thought
He'd seen the Saviour –
But it was his own blood,
Drawn by misbehaviour.

"You stupid old bugger,
Look what you've made me do,"
He seethed with phlegm and rage.
"This is because of you."

He mixed his young red blood
With the monastic dust
Then turned to face the wall
And stabbed and bled and cussed.

Was it retribution
Sent down from up above?
The nun said He sees all
Combining fear with love.

' Infinity? OK!
But two eyes seeing all? '
Well that was a theory
That made no sense at all.

' Perhaps there is a God.
A kind of local cop
But who they overlooked
The day they shut up shop? '

"Would you like a tissue
To wipe the blood away?"
"Listen, mate," he snapped back.
"Be careful what you say."

"Are you a Catholic?"
I asked the irate youth,
Who nurture and nature
Had trained to be uncouth.

He ignored the question
And filled his name with blood.
"This was my school," I said,
"Where caning was the rule."

"They caned yer, with a stick?
You should ' ave sent 'em down
For friggin ' GBH,"
The youth said with a frown.

"They used the cane and strap
Without fail everyday."
Now the boy was listening
To what I had to say.

"I wouldn't stand for that,"
The youth said with a grunt.
"If they tried it on me
I'd butt the stupid cunt."

"I think it did us good.
It taught us wrong from right
And we rubbed on the resin
To take away the bite."

"We also had prayers three
Or four times everyday.
In here or at the desk
We'd close our eyes and pray.

Do you support the church?"
I asked the shabby youth.
"I'm like me dad and mam,
A Man. United fan."

Like a boy I once knew
He looked familiar.
Even his ragged clothes
Seemed strangely similar:

Half the woollen goalposts,
And scuffed brown shoes worn thin
From kicking cobblestones
And tearing naked skin.

When the youth departed
I heard the black priesthood
Chanting in the Latin
That no one understood.

A place of deep shadows,
Confessionals at night,
But when the roof collapsed,
The worshippers saw the light.

I left the past behind,
Content that I'd survived,
And passed through spaces where
The Sanctus-bell had thrived.

Streets that once housed people
Who coughed the same stale air,
Cowed beneath the long rod,
And lived on hope and prayer.

RHYMING SHORT STORIES

AMORE

This green oasis they call a municipal park
(but with exclusions like NO ADMISSION AFTER DARK)
was built to remind the industrial working-class
that the world was not all concrete grey – but trees and grass

where creaking swings and roundabout on sharp gravel base
taught children how to handle the sight of blood with grace
and comprehend biology at advanced level
or assess opposing concepts like God and devil.

But the Church and Council deemed the park a place where lust
and fornication could flourish freely after dusk;
so before the war they built railings around the park
and locked the gates every night, ten minutes before dark.

In 1940, the bars were removed, it was said,
to make ammunition from the iron and the lead,
and, unregulated, the park stayed open all night
for lovers to copulate in comfort, out of sight.

But by then the local men had gone away to war,
and up the hill, close to the park, huts were built to store
those Italian prisoners of war who'd arrived
via land and sea, sentenced to spend their time inside.

By 1945 they had made themselves at home
and, with misguided authority, allowed to roam
with the few housewives who were more than willing to please,
while their soldier-husbands were clearing up overseas.

Now sex was a subject taboo until twelve in class,
but outside of school before our time and in the grass
or concealed like commandos by foliage and leaves,
we studied close-up or with a bird's-eye view from trees

as the housewife and enemy crossed the sloping field
to the dark corner of the park where, (they thought) concealed
from prying eyes, they'd communicate by touch and sound.
We held our breath up in the branches and on the ground

and watched them walk towards us, seemingly unattached –
but in a line she followed him to the flat grass patch
where she placed her red Sunday coat, lining to the ground.
Tenderly, her POW friend lowered her down.

"Amore," he whispered to Mrs Brown. "Amore."
The same word he'd used the day before with Mrs Grey.
"Oh, go on, Luigi. Not just yet. You are a pest."
"Amore," he said, his hand between her blouse and vest.

*"Luigi! You Italians are fast. Don't rush me;
you'll be giving me 'iccups. I've not long since 'ad tea."*
"Amore," he said again, his lips on her neckscarf
beneath which, two days before, his mate had left his mark.

"Don't, please. I've got a sore throat," she lied, moving his hand
from off her chest and rearranging the tight neckband,
a modified scarf, that concealed Antonio's love-
bites. And, unobserved, we watched from bushes and above.

"Listen, Luigi; don't go thinking I'm a sex maniac."
"Amore," he said, laying Mrs Brown on her back.
She put her hands behind her head and said: *" You Ities
turn me on with yer boot-black 'air and come-to-bed eyes."*

"Amore," he repeated, with a hand on her knee.
"Amore! Don't you know any English, Luigi?"
Luigi shook his head and moved his hand up her skirt.
Mrs Brown uncrossed her naked legs and lay inert.

Like students encircling the operating table,
it was mobile anatomy that we were able
to analyse, and with bated breath and racing heart
we watched as Mrs Brown slowly moved her legs apart.

Mr Bert Brown was still abroad and wearing khaki,
but Mrs Brown's thoughts were on the colour green, the tree
to be precise, where she'd seen a movement in the leaves.
It took her a minute to recognise Eric Jeeves.

Eric, my pal, lived across the street from Mrs Brown,
and knowing he'd been spotted, decided to slide down
the tree and, without looking back, fled across the green,
while Mrs Brown pulled down her skirt and began to scream.

Improperly dressed in his POW grey suit,
Luigi sprang to his feet and took-off in pursuit,
and shouted: "You leetle swine. I'll slit your throat."
Confused, Mrs Brown buried her head beneath her coat.

With padded shoulders and skirts that climbed above the knee,
throughout that summer the ladies continued to see
their Latin lovers, Luigi and Antonio,
but now having to take turns with their neighbours, Lil and Flo.

Having impregnated Mrs Brown and Mrs Grey,
at the summer's end the POWs went away.
That year we had heard much talk of love (or amore),
but could only guess what Bert and Stan would have to say.

UNHOLY MOSES

Winter is about the dark streets
Where, in the summer gone, bleached sheets
Had billowed proud like tall-ship sails
Held high by goodwill and two nails.

Now the night streets shine like wet coal;
A stark symbol of this blackhole
Of foundries and wretching chimneys,
Trades unions and council laundries.

There's Psycho at the Rivoli,
Bingo and the Co-op divi,
Backstreet bookies and the Palais,
And for ten bob, short-time, Sally.

Welcome to our community.
This is your opportunity
To spend some time with a native
Who, by nature, is offensive.

This then's your night out with Moses.
No, not him. This one composes
And redefines his own history
Like a Conan Doyle mystery.

But first let me draw his picture:
Perfectly formed but miniature,
A little under five feet two
In a dark suit, shiny and blue.

A suit? Yes, but thirty years old
And worn in heatwaves or on cold
Winter's evenings with flannelette
Grey shirt buttoned up to his neck.

Born during 1895,
He's managed to reach sixty-five.
That's right: it's now 1960:
Marilyn Monroe and Presley.

To hear him talk, he's done it all,
But then he's as narrow as short.
Hates the Germans, Japs and Ities,
Black skin, lesbians and queer guys.

It's Castro and Cuba Libre,
Porgy and Bess at the opera,
Brezhnev and King – but that's not all:
There's also JFK and de Gaulle;

Space flights, black v white, the cold war,
Self-government for Singapore.
But Moses has no interest
In the never-ending unrest,

Unless it's happening on his street
Then he'll sort it out with two feet.
But we've only his word for that,
And as they say, he chews the fat.

Well, it is his birthday today,
With a full head of hair but grey,
And only one tooth in his mouth,
Tobacco stained from north to south.

This afternoon, with a mandate,
He claimed his pension on the State.
For five years he's been on the dole;
Same paymaster, different payroll.

Worked for forty-six years at more
Than sixty outdoor and indoor
Jobs, most within a short bus ride,
But "..don't come back," the foremen cried.

Claims to have worked in all the pubs
As well as cleaning downtown clubs,
And backyards of the well-to-do;
Swept the lion cage in the zoo!

But his working days are finished,
And when his house is demolished
Next year, he'll be moved to a flat.
" And that will be the end of that,"

He said. " Ten 'effin' miles away.
That'll be some friggin' birthday.
I was born opposite Belle Vue.
The council ' aven't got a clue!"

He is in a talkative mood;
Not about chores like cooking food -
Since his wife died ten years ago
He's become the local wino.

His monologue is historic,
Mixed freely with philosophic
One-liners based on crudity
But underlined with self-pity.

" Finished school at thirteen," he said,
Proud that the only thing he's read
Since, is the Mirror's racing page.
And this man thinks he's the pub's sage!

" Everything I know came from life,"
He enthuses, " and my dear dead wife."

I sense his beer is getting low.
" Would you like another drink, Mo?"

" I can't get you one back, you know.
Today I suffered a real blow."
He paused for affect but then said:
" Me gas meter was robbed by Ted."

" Ted?" the barman said in surprise.
" Your son? The one with the kind eyes?"

" Aye, did it wi ' me own 'ammer.
Mind, can't get work with that stammer."

" Thought you said 'e went to grammar,"
Questioned the barmaid, Miss Glamour.

" 'e was expelled," Moses explained,
Complaining about his backpain.
" Cheers, Bernie," he said, his loose lips
Sucking at the froth-laden drips
Sliding down the side of the jar.

" Look, you missed a drop, Grandpa,"
Miss Glamour said, scratching cleavage;
Her bleached hair piled high like bandage,
" Be squeezin' out the barmats next,"
She implied, sticking out her chest.

" 'ere, now don't be cheeky, young miss,"
Moses replied, " or you'll get this,"
He concluded with a hand on crotch.

" But first you'll need a drop of scotch,"
Moses' son, Ted, said, crisp and clear
With no hint of stammer or fear
Such as you'd expect from a thief
Who'd caused his father so much grief.
" Happy birthday and retirement,"
Ted said, arm around his parent
While taking a clean five pound note
From his Harris tweed overcoat.
" It's whisky all around tonight.
Last week, me racing bets came right.
Drink and be merry, it's my treat."

Moses stared at his size four feet.

A WALK ON THE WILD SIDE

Joe didn't expect much from life.
He'd never planned to take a wife,
But while out strolling in the park
He came on Freda in the dark
With hoisted skirt and tattooed shark.

Soon Freda began to inflate
And the vicar from his pulpit
Consigned the pair to lifelong hate.
But it wasn't spermicidal
And young Joe was suicidal.

So he drank his wages everyday
Did Joe McCan, the railway man,
On black and tan in oil-stained serge
He sat in the pub where he smoked
And cursed - but couldn't quench his thirst.

By fifty, Freda had grown thin
With long black hair and yellow skin,
And rain or shine she always wore
The great-coat from the First World War
She'd purchased at the Army store.

On Friday nights the railway man
Was at his peak and drank ten pints,
Ate pickled eggs and Parmesan,
Smoked twenty cigarettes or more,
Played darts but couldn't keep the score.

On Saturdays, with silver coins
In her purse, and with Joe in bed,
Freda went to see the astute
Pawnshop man, and quietly said:
" ' ave come for Joe's best Sunday suit. "

They lived on a street of two up
And down with dust, damp and decay;
But with advice from a neighbour,
One day she asked for extra pay –
" Or else I'll withdraw me labour. "

Joe reacted and shouted, " Whore, "
And knocked poor Freda to the floor.
Cursing his inebriation
She felt alone and insecure
But promised retaliation.

It was a hot day when Freda,
Wrapped in her khaki overcoat
Finally emerged on her way
To the corner grocery shop
For a small loaf and one lamb-chop.

The McCans had no history.
Where they came from was a mystery,
But like the take-aways in Crewe
(And Freda's weekly IOU)
The McCan family grew and grew.

Well, that's the introduction done;
Now it's time to move on and write
In some detail about one night
When the temperature was high
And Joe was mixing hops with rye.

With a depleting wage packet
In his railway-issue jacket,
Joe'd spent five hours at the Torbay
Arms, beside the railway station
Suffering wind and train vibration.

In those days the pubs stopped serving
At thirty minutes after ten
Except for those few unswerving
Experts of imbibing like Len
And Ken, two other railway men.

They were allowed five minutes more
To drink the dregs and flick their ash
On the men-only, beer-stained floor
Before staggering, short of cash,
To urinate outside the door.

But no matter how much Joe drank
He remained a punctual man
Leaving his inebriate mates
Vomiting by the gas-works' gates,
And went home on the day's last tram.

All the back streets in the ghetto
(Described as the rear door to hell)
Looked the same in the dark, but Joe
Navigated by sound and smell,
Listening to his hobnails echo.

That night, the street was deathly quiet
But the youth against the lamp-post
Flicked a fag-end, glowing red,
And spat a mouthful on Joe's coat.
" You dirty little sod, " Joe said.

" ' Ere, watch it, mate, or I'll smash yer, "
The youth replied, drawing phlegm
And preparing to spit again.
" Wipe it off me coat, " Joe demanded;
But the strange youth countermanded:

" Wipe it off yerself, you fat slob. "
" I'm warning you, " Joe shouted back,
But aware the young maniac
Was about to throw another gob.
" Wipe it off or I'll give you a crack. "

The youth spat again and the phlegm
Fell on Joe's boot. Joe raised his fist
But the youth laughed: " You're Brahms and Liszt. "
" I'll show you, you, you dirty louse, "
Joe stuttered, falling in the house.

Whether it was the hot weather
Or interaction between foe
And beer, we'll perhaps never know,
But Joe, stripped to socks and string-vest,
Leaned over and touched Freda's breast.

She went berserk and shouted rape
And threw the piss-pot in his face.
In her ex-army sleeping-coat
She ran downstairs in naked feet
And stopped the policeman on the street.

" ' e tried to rape me, officer. "
" Who did? " the policeman replied,
Questioning who would acquiesce
And want to touch such ugliness.
" Me 'usband, that's who, " Freda cried.

When the policeman climbed the stairs
Joe seemed to be asleep in bed.
" Looks peaceful, " the constable said.
But in his imagination,
Joe was planning strangulation...

THE MENAGERIE

" Pint of mild beer, please, " said Percy Woodlark,
red faced from his short walk across the park,
the only patch of green for half a mile,
attracting the kids and odd paedophile.
Not that Percy was of that persuasion;
let's get it straight: he was not one to swan
at night near the public lavatory
with a hard-on and the mandatory
fistful of silver and ankle-length coat
on the look-out for a willing deep throat.

Percy was small of stature and polite
with a preference for toast and Marmite –
but his wife? Well, she was a different case:
beneath that front of lavender and lace
she'd vibrate daily with a hidden need,
yet made Percy go to the pub when he'd
rather sit in front of the fire and doze.

" Why do you have to dress in your best clothes
on a Sunday morning when you're cleaning? "
Percy asked, more to himself than with meaning.
But Mrs Woodlark ignored the question
with the retort that such a suggestion
implied that in the week she looked a mess.
Percy blushed and put on his long-sleeved vest.

It was always on a Sunday midday,
at twelve-thirty to be exact, she'd say:
" Go on Percy, time for you to visit
the Coach, and be sure one pint's your limit,
and don't come ' ome till after two, " she said,
" I need some peace and quiet to cure me ' ead. "

Percy was worried about the headpain
his wife suffered every Sunday - from strain,
he thought, recalling the night before when
she said: not now, me ' ead's at it again.

It was not in his nature to defy
her word and, in flat cap and soup-stained tie,
he walked down to the local drinking den
where he sat listening to the noisy men
who laughed and talked in tobacco smoke
about fornication and womenfolk -
the same way their forefathers used to joke.

Percy sat on the chair still hot from Frank,
the round-shouldered clerk from the Co-op Bank.

Meanwhile, outside the one o'clock Sunday
public house where shiny suits and decay
polluted the air with conversation,
Bill Brown, alert but in contemplation
(fortified earlier with a double scotch),
leaned on the wall and studied his watch.
Dusted down with talc, Bill felt spick-and-span
in his dark blue suit, red shirt and cyan
tie, grinning ear to ear to expose
the gap between his front teeth where he chose
to hold the thin cigarette that glowed red
with each inhalation and when he said:
" ' ad yer end away lately, Frank, old lad? "
with his preference for all things gonad.

" Nowt down for me, Bill. Sorry can't stop, "
Frank replied, going in the corner shop,
and emerging with two bottles of brown
ale he shuffled across the shantytown
of back-to-backs and factory chimney stack
that spewed out carbon dioxide and black
dust to cover the washing on the line
of a sardine neighbourhood in decline.

Although Bill was bright and Percy sullen,
the two men had a lot in common:
Bill was a coalman who left his trademark
on the underwear of Mrs Woodlark;
but naive Percy was a chimney-sweep,
and while all the neighbours in the street
knew that Percy's wife was Bill Brown's lover,
Bill's weekday dust was his undercover.

" These fags'll be the death of me, " Bill complained
to himself, the smoke covering his ingrained
face. He spat out the cigarette, rolling
another to take its place, and strolling
in the direction of the Woodlarks' address
where, with Percy in the pub, he'd caress
Mrs Woodlark with hands that left no trace -
except for the smile he put on her face.

By now, Bill's long-suffering wife, Abigail,
was on her second bottle of brown ale,
and bouncing up and down in bed with Frank,
the round-shouldered clerk from the Co-op Bank.

With apologies to those readers unsympathetic to naked breasts and haute couture. No apology is offered to ...

THE OFFICIAL RECEIVER

for Harry

" I'm from the Official Receiver's office,"
Said the young woman in black skirt but topless
At the internal door to the Chairman's suite
On the first floor overlooking the main street.

The Chairman, in dark blue suit and silver tie,
Held out a manicured hand to signify
A courteous welcome, trying to ignore
The dead match she flicked to the carpeted floor.

" This is a non-smoking office. I propose
You put it out." But the smoke streamed down her nose.
On the street below, a flautist played the tune
That he played every Monday afternoon.

Tall and round, she lifted the hem of her skirt,
Scratched a fishnet knee and began to assert
That authority delegated in her
To intimidate any entrepeneur.

" I'll sit there," she said, pointing to where he sat.
" And now we will have a little friendly chat,"
She whined on, from the waist naked at his desk.
' If this is a wind-up,' he thought, ' it's grotesque.'

" Excuse me... but," the Chairman began, thinking
He should explain her state, but she was drinking
The cold tea remaining in his flowered cup.
Dribbling, she said: " I'm in charge. Don't push your luck."

" I am the Chairman," he replied, turning red.
" Don't raise your voice to me," the Receiver said,
Leaning forward and letting her bosom flop
Between the accoutrements on the desk top.

The Chairman was incensed by the callous way
Her drooping breasts brushed his pen and China tray.
Before he could get out what he had to say,
She said: "From hereon, it's me who you obey."

" Straight to the point; I've been brought in by the bank
Because you have stretched them, and to be quite frank
This company is not worth a paperclip,
And that's why you've been placed in receivership."

" Give me all your credit cards before we start,
And then I will examine your cash-flow chart,"
She said, swinging her body round from the hip
And sitting like the prow of a sailing ship.

But unsupported, a rose-tattooed breast caught
The gold-plated onyx box his staff had brought
And sent it flying off the desk. " Oh dear, dear !"
She said, spraying cheap perfume behind her ear.

" Don't stand there like a machine-minder's oilcan.
Pick them up," she demanded of the Chairman,
Stubbing out her cigarette in the saucer.
' I suppose,' he thought, ' she's somebody's daughter.'

On this presumption, he picked up the fragments
And carefully placed them with the ornaments
And family picture on the window ledge
While the Receiver continued to allege

That the reason for the company's demise
Was because he had been skating on thin ice
And skimming the cream off the top of the milk
So he could live a life of diamonds and silk.

" Before you go any further would you note,
I would like you to put on a blouse or coat,"
The Chairman said, and the Receiver shouted:
" How dare you tell me what to wear," and flouted

Her chest by inhaling deeply and sweeping
Up her breasts, declared: " This style is in keeping
With the latest trend - but you wouldn't know that.
Okay, back to business. Let me see the vat."

' Even if you had a rose bush on your tit,'
The Chairman thought, distracted from the profit
And loss discussion, ' You would still be ugly.'
" Why do you think I am here? " she asked smugly.

" I haven't got a clue," the Chairman replied.
" I've stole nothing. Haven't committed homocide;
Still within my agreed overdraft level,
And then you turn up like a topless devil."

" Things like these don't come cheap," the woman gloated.
" You listen to what I say: I'm a devoted
Follower of fashion. This came from Paris;
So can I get on with my analysis? "

" Since you say the bank has frozen my account,
And withdrawn my overdraft, it's tantamount
To closing down my business. I can't oppose
What you say, but I wish you'd put on some clothes."

" Hear this: how I dress has got absolutely
Nowt to do with you, " she said, resolutely.
" I suppose your accounts are like a jigsaw,"
She continued, opening the desk's top drawer.

" Now where do you keep the bank paying-in book?
I do hope you don't turn out to be a crook,"
She drolled on without pausing to take a breath.
" Some of the accounts I see scare me to death!"

" Would you please take your hand out of my drawer,"
The Chairman requested politely, " Before
I phone your office and lodge a complaint
About your attitude and lack of restraint."

" May I remind you," she replied haughtily,
" That you have no desk. You are up a gum tree,
And the sooner you come to terms with your plight,
The better. It's no use getting uptight."

" The books are in the top drawer," he explained,
Leaning on the desk and studying the veined
Lines and small tattoo on the woman's left breast,
Like a rose on a street map of the North West.

Only then did the Chairman appreciate
That the aim of fashion is to titillate.
" Move away; keep your distance. I need more space,"
She cried, rummaging inside a make-up case.

The Chairman made a note of her reaction
And, in what at first had been a distraction,
In the visiting woman's capriciousness
Identified what he thought was a weakness.

But, as so often happens, embarrassment
Turned to anger and misguided harassment.
Reappearing from behind the Max Factor lid
She slowly peeled a banana and studied

The expression on the Chairman's averted face,
And chewing banana said: " You're a disgrace
For letting your business get in such a mess.
You've been creaming. Come on, confess."

In four bites she ate the fruit and threw the skin
With tremendous force in the waste-paper bin.
And through the last mouthful, called for the chequebook.
Taking the chequebook from his pocket he shook

It across her breasts and the cool draught of air
Caused her nipples to expand. " Don't you dare stare,"
She shouted, holding her hands before her chest.
But the Chairman responded: " You've been well-blessed."

" You can't speak to me like that. I'm not something
The cat dragged in," she said, fingering her ring
On the middle finger of her embraced hand.
I need to freshen up. Where is the washstand?"

While the Receiver was out of the office,
He opened a window on the prognosis
That a constant flow of cold air directed
At the chair would keep her nipples erected.

" Is there a draught ?" she asked, returning to the chair.
" I've lowered the temperature of the air,
To help you reduce the running costs, " he lied,
Watching her nipples as they solidified.

And the street map on her bosom changed from black
To blue with goose-flesh spreading from front to back.
Conscious of the movement on her chest, she crossed
Her arms – but her former composure was lost.

" I can't see any sign of insolvency
In these accounts, and there's no discrepancy
Such as they described at the bank last Friday.
I must say I can't see the talked-of disarray."

The Chairman was pleased with what she had to say.
His order book was full and assets okay.
Why would the institution want to foreclose
By sending a woman with no upper clothes?

He stood transfixed on the blood-red rose tattoo
But he was confused why the bank would persue
This policy when he'd survived aggression
And more than one State imparted recession.

" What's this name here on the chequebook?" she enquired,
Arms across her chest as modesty required.
" Harry Smith Tour Company," the Chairman said.
" Well where," she asked, " is the book for Harry's Bread?"

" I haven't got a clue. Try the upper floor,
Unit two. There's no need to knock at the door."
" No need to knock? That's not my style," she replied.
" They've been gone two weeks," the Chairman clarified.

He smiled as the topless woman in high shoes
Struggled towards the door, trying to excuse
Her confusion. " And don't forget this, " he said,
Wrapping the banana skin around her head.

As incredible as it may seem, in the nineteen sixties, topless fashion was promoted by the media and, for a short period, a minority of women walked the streets with naked breasts. On continental beaches it continues today.

THE SKULL

It was late evening of a winter's night
As I sat alone in my living-room
Safe from the north wind and deepening gloom
I sat by myself in my twilight room.

I sat by myself in my twilight room
On a rocking-chair with a warming drink
And listened to the rain on the window pane
Rat-a-tat-tatting like a willow cane
But I felt secure on Cemetery Lane.

But I felt secure on Cemetery Lane
In my tied-cottage by the graveyard gate
On the ancient hill were the wind spat hail
And the dead were buried in nylon voile,
For I was the digger of clay and soil.

For I was the digger of clay and soil
But rat-a-tat-tat was the rain's refrain
As it tapped repeatedly on my window pane
And the gale-force wind hammered on my door
As I paced around my paving-stone floor.

As I paced around my paving-stone floor
I closed the curtains to silence the storm
That rattled the windows and shook the stair
While the fire's reflections danced on the wall
And I fell asleep in my rocking chair.

And I fell asleep in my rocking chair
But then a knocking came into my dream
And the smell of soil crept under the door
And the floorboards creaked in an upper room
It was then that I heard the piercing scream.

It was then that I heard the piercing scream,
A cry of such pain that my blood ran cold
And I felt concern for the fearful soul
Out in the graveyard with the tombs and stones
And all I could think of was blood and bones.

And all I could think of was blood and bones
As I stepped outside but the lane was still
Except for the rain on my window sill
And the fox that crept to its hillside lair
So I shuffled back to my fireside chair.

So I shuffled back to my fireside chair
Where I wrapped myself in an eiderdown
And I covered my ears from the storm-tossed sound
That blew arctic cold on a matt-black night
And a skull appeared in the fireside light.

And a skull appeared in the fireside light
And moved like a shadow across the room.
With a stare that fastened me to my chair
And a dust-dry smile as wry as the moon
The skull drifted around my living room.

The skull drifted around my living room
As I fought to wake from the fretful dream
Where hollow black eyes could see without sight
But some invisible force held me down
While the skull told me of a burning town.

While the skull told me of a burning town
And quantified the day's dead and the dying.
I wanted to run but could not escape
From the structure of bone and attitude
That talked fluidly of torture and rape.

That talked fluidly of torture and rape
And how decay and destruction began;
It revealed those places on earth called hell
And soon I was falling under the spell
Of the floating skull with a tale to tell.

Of the floating skull with a tale to tell;
It spoke at length of devastation,
Those terrible acts of God not Satan,
Thousands of dead was the estimation
Said the waxen skull in conversation.

Said the waxen skull in conversation,
That was so knowledgeable and precise,
The unwanted messenger of death and vice
That knew all the answers to time and place,
And the shock-waves flowed from its flattened face.

And the shock-waves flowed from its flattened face
When I asked how it knew about living
But continued to talk about dying,
And said it was death not life that consumed
The apparition in my living-room.

The apparition in my living-room
Began to guess and opinionate
About abstractions at some future date,
And I questioned the truth and confusion
Of the latest visiting illusion.

Of the latest visiting illusion.

It was midnight when the skull departed
After stripping my soul and senses bare,
And I stood alone in my living-room
But something was moving my rocking-chair,

But something was moving my rocking-chair...

The author of the novel *BOREALANUS*, with total lack of judgement, gave a copy of the book to his ageing aunt.

CATHY

" The novel is not about family,"
I told my dead mother's sister, Cathy
Who lives alone in a flat-type attic
Surrounded by blacks, and xenophobic.

" It starts in nineteen twenty-six," I said,
" And most of the characters are now dead."
" I was only a girl then," she replied,
That was when we first went to the seaside.

" Yer mam and me and yer granddad and gran
Went to Blackpool and we 'ad chips and scran.
I can remember it like yesterday:
Went by chara and driver lost 'is way."

" Some names may sound familiar," I explained,
Wondering how Cathy would view the maimed
Ex-soldier called Will from the First World War,
Like her own dad, henpecked and battle-sore.

" She 'ad lovely legs, yer mam. Should 'ave been
A dancer, she should. When she was fourteen
The boys used to whistle 'er on the street;
But she wouldn't stand cheek from a deadbeat.

" Are you leaving this book for me to read?"
She asked, an inhaler helping her breathe
Easier, having just said more than she'd
Said all week. " Yes, it's for you, " I agreed.

" I can't read much more than a page a day.
It's not about sex that they seem to play
On the TV everyday, is it?
Meself, I prefer a good whodunit."

I explained it was a tale of decay;
About those grey streets where she used to play
And where she had lived for eighty-three years.
A tale of survival, laughter and tears.

" What decay is that?" she asked with a frown,
Her thin neck stretching from her dressing gown
Of faded flowers buttoned to the chin.
She seemed to have forgotten the vermin.

" Don't you recall the beetles in the hearth,
The flagged backyard with the coal and tin bath?
Kneeling in the cold with the Evening News
Trying to light a fire. Holes in the shoes?"

" It wasn't like that," she said with a smile
That suggested my recall was facile.
" We kept the tin bath on a nail in shed,
And dad made the fire while I was in bed."

' Somebody had to make the fire,' I thought,
' With bits of wood and paper for support.
And boil the water on the fireside hob,
Then draw the blind for Saturday night's swab.'

" Don't you remember those back-alley screams
That could have been outside or in your dreams?
The drunks falling about in the shadows;
The spluttering gaslight and the psychos?"

" I 'ope you 'aven't written that stuff down,"
She said, with serious concern for her town.
" We've got Sunny Brow and other nice parks -
An 'in our street we 'ad two town 'all clerks!

" We 'ad real good neighbours when I was small,"
She said, with pride, but I seemed to recall
The walls were so thin, you heard neighbours fart.
And there was more than one street-corner tart.

Of course, with deference to her sex and age,
I considered it wise not to engage
In that debate, keeping thoughts in my head
That may be best written and left unsaid.

" It was boiled egg and bread for Thursday's tea?"
I said. " And my mother used to feed me
With bread and dripping, and that other treat:
Through to Wednesday eating Sunday's cold meat."

" We 'ad other things," she said with her frown.
" You could feed a family for 'alf-a-crown.
There was pig's trotters and tripe and cow-' eel.
None of our family ever missed a meal.

" If you've said we went without, it's not true.
I'm sorry; I don't want to upset you,
But you'll give some people the wrong idea,
Like thinkin' all the wages went on beer."

A high percentage of income was spent
On cigarettes and beer and, of course, rent,"
I replied, determined to put my side
Without any intention to misguide.

" Don't you remember, Cathy, how some lived?
As a kid I saw first-hand the squalid
Homes: stuffing out of chairs, ash in grate,
And how the council used to fumigate."

" That's news to me; never 'eard owt like that.
In all my life I've never seen a rat.
The roaches used to come in with the coal
But yer granddad kept them under control."

Her memory's sound. Perhaps she didn't know
How, when the toxic gas began to flow
From the van to the house next-door-but-two,
We stood outside because the fumes passed through.

" It was nowt to do with me what went on.
When I got 'ome from work the day was done.
I wore me treadlin' shoes six days a week,
And putting up me feet was Sunday's treat.

" In winter I didn't see a neighbour
For months on end. It was like 'ard labour
' avin' to make-up twelve dresses an hour
With me own feet switching on the power.

" It were toe down to go, ' eel down to stop,
All day long at that Manchester sweatshop.
Me poor legs felt just like two lumps of lead,
And that's probably why I never wed.

" Me fingers were sore and me eyes bloodshot."
" Twelve dresses an hour seems an awful lot,"
I suggested, studying her bent back.
" We worked in threes and you soon got the knack.

" With two sewers, I did the overlock;
And all day long we worked against the clock.
Yer mam worked with me before you was born
And we were on the tram at crack of dawn.

" After a quick breakfast of bread and jam,
We'd put on 'at and coat and get on tram.
Some went by bike and there were buses too.
You'd get up to a 'undred in the queue.

" The men went upstairs in their boilersuits,
Clattering up and down in 'obnail boots.
Upstairs you could cut the air with a knife.
When yer think, it was an un'ealthy life.

" A lot of water's gone under the bridge
Since yer dad brought yer granma a cabbage
When 'e 'd call courtin' yer mam after work,
And in the backyard 'is 'orse 'd go beserk."

" Why was that?" I asked, absorbing the past.
" It seemed to know when it 'ad done its last
Street call on the round selling fruit and veg.
And yer dad changed its name to Doll from Reg."

" I don't suppose it was pleased about that,"
I said, recalling a schoolboy called Pat.
" And yer mam didn't want to share 'er name
With an old Evening News 'orse, 'alf lame.

" It didn't stop 'er marryin' at all.
She got wed in white. There she is on wall."
It was the picture that hung on that hook
When I was young - since described in my book.

Like a tortoise coming out of its shell,
She stretched her neck and began to expel
Into her gaping mouth medication
That would help further clarification.

Would she recognise herself on the day
Of the wedding when the groom dressed in grey
Like my dad did for another photo
On that day more than sixty years ago?

For the purpose of the wedding alone,
I set that part in my grandparents' home
With the sister helping the bride prepare,
And her mother setting the tableware.

What have I done, letting her read the book?
It was in isolation that I took
That chapter away from the fictional
Characters who were unoriginal.

The bride's father has her father's real name!
To put the record straight I must explain,
If she finds any connection between
Fact and fiction, she has misread the scene.

Would it be paltry to make the excuse
That I need to take the book on the ruse
It is all about violence and sex
And politics, vengeance and decadence?

" It'll take me years to read all this novel.
It took months to read about the rabble
Who were riotin' in yer other book -
Although I'm not that keen on rats that cook."

She was flicking the pages and reading
A line here and there. I felt like pleading
For her to put the book on the knee-high
Table with her medicines and porkpie.

" Co-op?" she said, glasses before her face.
" Is that the one on 'yde road, the same place
Where we went to that wedding years ago
When yer dad was troubled with lumbago?

" 'ere, it was upstairs there we 'ad a 'am
Salad after we 'ad buried yer gran,
And we 'ad that great big room just to us,
And the undertaker made such a fuss."

On a cold and wet winter afternoon
Sitting in the middle of a ballroom
With paper tablecloth and serviette
Was not an occasion I could forget.

The previous Saturday afternoon -
When grandma had died in the living room -
Cathy, running around the house, went wild,
Screaming and shouting like a distraught child.

Now, ten years past her mother's final age
But imprisoned like a bird in a cage
By emphysema on an upper floor,
She lives alone with five locks on the door.

" That's much better," she said, patting her chest,
And replacing the spray can with the rest
Of her daily needs on the small table
By her side, *" but still unemployable."*

She smiled, and we looked behind each other's
Eyes. Her skin was stretched tight like her mother's
Face had been the year before she expired.
" How was the hospital trip?" I enquired.

" And what did they report about the test
They did on your waterworks and the rest
Of your problems down below the waistline?"
I asked, and she replied: *" She said it's fine."*

Quite separate from her emphysema,
She said the woman doctor had seen her
About the blood she found in her urine
And told her to halve the daily aspirin.

" I 'ad a funny turn on the table
And got so flustered I wasn't able
To take in what she said about me 'eart,
But I 'eard 'er say it would stop and start."

" Did she mean missing a beat?" I enquired.
" I'm not sure. I was excited and tired
An' lyin' 'alf naked in a strange room.
But she thought there was nowt wrong with me womb.

" The doctor said it was as good as new
As I've never 'ad sex. We didn't do
Things like that before marriage years ago;
So there'll be no wear and tear down below.

" I've not been right since they tried to break in."
Three months before, youths had attacked the thin
Front door with their feet until the door frame
Came away while they called her by her name.

It was the bolt screwed not to the frame but wall
That kept the gang on the communal hall.
" You should have dialled three nines," I said again,
But she said that would trouble the policemen.

" They knocked at first and asked to loan sugar,
But I shouted and said, go on, bugger
Off; and then they started battering the door.
I crawled under the bed and lay on floor."

I reassured her that with the deadlock
Set, it would be impossible to knock
The surrounding frame away from the wall
(I'd also put a camera in the hall).

She said the violence was worldwide and not
Just where she'd spent her life. *" There's not a lot*
You can do about it. They've got guns now.
I've 'eard they use them when they 'ave a row! "

What she had to say about guns was true,
But it was the poor parts where violence grew.
" They see it all on the tele, " she said.
" And single mums bringing up kids, I've read.

" There's no discipline in the schools these days,
The government's all talk and 'olidays,
Like those do-gooders who wouldn't live 'ere
For five minutes, never mind a full year.

" It'll get worse and then the police won't cope
With all the kids robbing and taking dope.
They've got a lot to answer, them MPs,
Allowin' in the so-called refugees.

" They know black and white can't live side by side;
That's why most of the blacks live in Moss side
And go around calling their kind, brother.
Strange, ' cause ' ere the whites can't stand each other."

Living alone, she had a lot to say,
And I wondered if when she knelt to pray
(As she said she'd done from the age of one),
She prayed for all the non-whites to begone.

Not only had she lost most of her peers,
Their replacements wear silk from shins to ears
Or pyjama trousers out on the street,
And add strange smelling spices to their meat.

" I wish I could turn back the clock, you know,
For a night out with yer mam at bingo.
Then we'd call at the Midland for a stout.
There'd be plenty for us to talk about."

On page 313 they're back together
In the pub sheltering from the weather;
One in a coat, the other in a mac,
For a pre-shopping Pale Ale and a snack.

Reading the novel may cause her distress
As it wouldn't be hard for her to guess
The cameo roles the family play
Against a landscape of industrial grey.

" Do you mind if I take the book away?
I'll bring it back when I come next Sunday."
I said the last sentence with fingers crossed -
But on Cathy, the words I said were lost.

She was somewhere I couldn't comprehend;
Perhaps at the Ritz with her Yankee friend.
Yankee friend? How could I have forgotten
About him. I suddenly felt rotten.

During the war she had an American
Friend who was shot down on an African
Mission. Only twice had I heard it said,
The plane went down with all hands in the Med.

I was a child when I first saw her cry
For that victim of war: her own G.I.
It was rumoured that's why she didn't wed.
Whatever the reason, she never said.

Thoughtlessly I had rewritten history
That she wouldn't find complimentary.
What was I thinking to bring her this book?
Perhaps her Yankee beau would have said, ' schnook '.

I hope that hero did not have the same
Name as the G.I.'s in the book called Cane
And Denver. That would be going too far
And akin to reading her own memoir.

" You can 'ave it back when I've finished it, "
She said, offering me a tea biscuit.
" I'll ignore all the sex and violence. "
She had a look of quiet defiance.

I watched my old aunt sitting in her chair,
Devalued like one of a broken pair -
But capable of talking with those dead
Members of her own family, she said.

She was turning the pages in the book
And, although intelligent, had the look
Of a woman much older than her years,
Alone with memories and souvenirs.

But I knew she was once one of a pair
Of beauties with black berets and blonde hair
And I can still see them in forty-eight
When arm-in-arm they seemed to illustrate

That the war was over and winter done.
There was the excitement of things to come,
And like the roadside blossom in mixed hues,
The sun brought out cotton frocks and white shoes.

A ten year old out of church with a crowd
En route to milkbar looked up and was proud
To meet relatives getting off the tram.
" Look, it's our Bernard, " Cathy said to mam,

Laughing as though they would live forever
And, according to Cathy, together
One day, as children again, they will be.
But where, in afterlife, will that leave me?

Will those reflections in the pages on
Her knee take her back to those days long gone?
Does she, I wonder, remember the time
When the child saw the sisters in their prime?

" Your mam and dad would 'ave been proud of you
With yer published books. She didn't 'ave a clue,
Yer mam said, 'ow yer became a poet.
D ' yer think we're all poets but don't know it?"

Cathy's humour was still corny but intact
And she continued: *" Don't forget the fact*
That it's now too late to turn the clock back.
One day your government will all be black."

With head inclined and chin upon her chest,
She's fallen in a trance. She must be stressed,
I thought, studying the novel that lay
Open on her knees, an arm's length away.

I dismissed the crass thoughts, crossing the room
To the sideboard with its bills, brush and comb
And framed pictures of the living and dead,
Including gran and granddad when they wed.

She standing in frilly blouse and drawn waist;
He sitting, with flying collar and chaiste.
In the sideboard mirror I saw my face
And suddenly I'd taken granddad's place.

" You've upset me," Cathy said from behind.
She hadn't fallen asleep but inclined
Her head to read the same page several times.
" We never committed them kind of crimes."

" Crimes? What crimes?" I asked in all innocence.
" Books last for years," she said in annoyance.
" The machinists didn't steal cloth like you've
Written. I'm sorry but I disapprove.

" Why, you've even named the place where I worked."
I felt the antagonism would get worse
And I could already sense the outrage
When she reached the wedding reception page.

" Why don't you apply for a groundfloor place?"
I said, trying not to look at her face.
" I'd never be able to sleep at night.
Don't worry about me. I'll be all right."

Cathy's response was emphatic and she
Had conditioned herself not to foresee
Beyond the next meal. " With a ground-floor flat
You could walk down to the shops for a chat."

" Even if I could get to the shops, they're
All boarded, and anyway, I don't care
For going out for a bit of mince meat
With those hooligans out there on the street."

" How's the breathing?" I asked, as she inhaled.
" I'm still doin ' it?" she said, and exhaled
Her medication as she gasped for air,
Muttering her usual 'save-me-God' prayer.

Like an old frayed photograph, she stood at
The dark window of her OAP flat
And waved, holding my novel in her hand.
An ageing lady in a foreign land.

TWO WEEKS LATER

"I'm driving past the Longsight street market
And should be at your door in a minute,"
I said to Cathy, the phone at my head,
Watching a black man eat a stick of bread.

Longsight was a district once white and poor.
It still seemed poor but the whites were fewer,
And while most of the buildings looked the same,
The flavour was now curry and chowmein.

"I'll be behind the door to let you in,"
She replied, but sounding like stone on tin.
Either she had inhaled her medicine
Or was about to dish out discipline.

"Are you okay?" I said, stopped at the lights
Where the coloured skins outnumbered the whites
By a ratio of thirteen to two,
And the posters, like the talk, were Urdu.

"Yes," she replied, but with less emphasis.
The tone of her voice said something was amiss.
"I'll put the kettle on. Do you want tea
Or are you still drinking that black coffee?"

"Still on the antibiotics," I said,
As the traffic lights changed to green from red
And a group in saris and pantaloons
Hurried by with helium-filled balloons.

Cathy was dressed from head to toe in black
Confirming that I was in for some flack.
"I'll go to the lav now I've let you in,"
She said, turning like paint-chipped porcelain.

The novel was on the knee-high table
With bookmark in place and I was able
To see what I thought was page one three nine.
So far in the book in such a short time!

When the cistern flushed, I put the book down
And she returned to her chair with a frown.
"When I get me breath, I'll get you a cup."
Her expression confirmed something was up.

"You've upset me again, writing all that."
Able to guess what was coming, I sat
On the opposite chair and asked what she meant.
"I'm very un'appy with that comment."

"Look, Cathy; I've told you, it's all fiction,"
I said, attempting to put conviction
In my denial of what she may say.
"It's imagination. Like a stage play."

"See what you've written on page one five five.
You can't say that's imagination. I've
Never read anything so 'orrible."
About yer granma. It's deplorable."

"Cathy, please don't take it to heart," I sighed.
"That woman in the book's not her," I lied.
She leaned forward with her body in space
And an unusual look crossed her face.

"I thought you were only on one three nine?"
"It's there, right under 1939,"
She shouted. I could see it was hopeless.
"In 'er forties, 'er mother was toothless.."

She held the open book close to her face
And said what I'd written was a disgrace.
"..'er thin and colourless lips painted red
With peach rouge on each cheek," aloud she read.

".. Short 'air-like creases lined 'er upper lip."
I knew I was in for an awkward trip.
"And this bit's about me dad, I presume:
..'is war-injured leg stretched into the room.

"That's me mam and dad and don't deny it.
Not only that, and you'll 'ave to admit,
I'm Eve, one of the sisters who may be,
According to you, 'avin' a baby!

"What will the neighbours say? They'll think it's me.
I'd better go an' make a cup of tea,
And take an Aspro to settle me 'eart.
What you've written 'as given me a start."

"Make mine a black coffee, please. With one spoon,"
I said, as Cathy shuffled from the room,
Bowed and scratching an exposed collarbone.
I sat back, grateful to be left alone.

And thankful I hadn't described the love scene
Between Eve and Herbert after they'd been
To see Clark Gable and Carole Lombard,
And how she conceived in the old churchyard.

In the past, that would have filled a whole page
But I don't want to contemplate the rage
That my old aunt Cathy would undergo
Had her fictional image stooped so low.

If platonic text has caused such disquiet,
I'm sure detailed sex would cause a riot,
For she is much more alert than I thought --
And she's yet to meet her Yankee escort!

Cathy once owned a two-up and two-down
On the northside of the same Gorton town
But she was rehoused by a clerk's decree
And allocated a council flat key.

Now you might think that a working-class town
Is one shade of grey, but that is unsound
Philosophy as any back-street kid
Will say: the shades range from sour to putrid.

From the soot-black Victorian terraced
Houses with their small dark rooms and fibrous
Cobwebs, paint-splashed between wall and ceiling,
With six decades of flowered paper peeling,

And their peculiar smell of methane.
To those rows less tarnished by acid rain,
And with two extra cubic feet of air
But still back-to-back and in disrepair.

And then there's the red-bricked semi-detached
Council houses with their walled-off and thatched
Front gardens growing the odd broken chair,
And neighbours with their 'don't-look-at-me' stare.

"Are you sure you don't want some milk in it?"
She asked, spilling coffee on the carpet
From the chipped cup rattling on the saucer.
"It looks just like a cup of black water."

"United played badly today," I said.
"I think they're overpaid and overfed.
One's on fifty thousand a week," she cried,
Placing the beverage on the tiled fireside.

"That's more than I earned in forty-nine years.
There's no justice in this world. It brings tears
To me eyes," she continued. *"And they claim*
It's talent, but it's only a kid's game."

Thankfully, her mind was off the novel
And she began to rant how immoral
For someone to make in one week what she
Earned working from fourteen to sixty-three.

"And another thing," she said, changing tack.
"When we went shopping, yer mam wore a mac
And I wore the coat. Of course you knew that;
But 'ow did you know about the lilac

"Flowers yer mam carried when she got wed?"
Looking at the picture above her head
Of the young woman with lilacs and lace,
I put an innocent look on my face.

"What flowers and coats are you talking about?"
"I'm not daft; I can see family throughout
Yer book. You've even put the groom in grey
And described the street and back alleyway.

"It's just like it used to be before they
Pulled the 'ouses down – and didn't they say
It was to make way for a wider road,
And then shipped us all off by the cart-load?

"Well it was nearly thirty years ago
They moved all those families to Wilmslow,
And my employer was ten miles away;
So when yer granddad died, I moved back this way.

"And I 'ear the road's the same as it was
Except there are fields. It's funny, because
They built a petrol station on a green
Where, in those days, no grass or cars 'ad been.

"It used ter be shanks's pony or bike –
Although the bus service was very good; not like
I 'ear it is today now it's private
Where the only thing that counts is profit.

"By the way, I've never seen a man crawl
Down the street like that man who seems to fall
In yer book everytime 'e's 'ad a drink.
That's in your imagination, I think."

"It's fact. There was a man who, without fail,
Would crawl home after a night on the ale.
Yet when he went to work he looked quite smart
In the standard uniform of a clerk.

"Different alcohols affect the brain
In ways that vary between hop and grain.
Or, in the case of legs, that decider
Whether one walks or falls: scrumpy cider."

*"Scrumpy cider? Whether it's true or not
I think you've made it all up, like a lot
Of what you've written. And I say your view
Of your granma, me mam, is just not true."*

"I'm not going all over that again."
*"No, because you're embarrassed and when
You write about the ex-prisoner of war
As being called Will, you've said it all."*

"When you read on, you'll see it's not your dad.
The man in the book called Will has a bad
Chest, caused by too much smoking, but the cough
Turns to emphysema and sees him off."

Cathy rearranged herself in the chair
And looked in my eyes with that wide-eyed stare.
Without thinking, I'd raised her condition,
Caused not by fags, but toxic emission.

*"When I was young, they called it bronchitis.
Everybody seemed to 'ave an itis.
There was appendicitis, arthritis,
Laryngitis and that dermatitis*

*"That you'd see on the backs of people's 'ands;
And the laryngitis affected the glands
Up 'ere in the throat. Could 'ave been the smoke.
Everybody was burning coal and coke.*

*"We were living on top of each other.
It's a wonder we didn't all smother
In those pea-soupers that used to come down
And were so thick you couldn't see the ground.*

"D'yer remember those fogs? They were yellow
And so thick and foul you couldn't swallow.
And when you put an 'anky to yer face
It turned black like the back of the fireplace."

"Yes, I recall getting lost in the fog –
Or smog – and feeling as sick as a dog.
Hearing fog signals and next door croaking
From carbon monoxide and chain-smoking."

"In winter all the people 'ad bad chests.
That's why we'd wear woollen scarves and vests,
And you could wrap the scarf around yer 'ead.
But a lot of neighbours finished up dead.

"If the cause of death was on those 'eadstones
It'd tell a story of 'ow those bones
Went to the cemetery before their due,
Because of so-called bronchitis and flu.

"When I was a girl, the men wore black suits
And flat caps on Sunday with lace-up boots,
An' yer'd see them walkin' to the public
'ouse like smokin' chimneys with asthmatic

"Chests and backs bent as they coughed up black phlegm.
It was the smoke that put many of them
In an early grave, but they didn't know
That they would die from in'alin' tobacco."

"And it was more addictive in those days,"
I said. "And the smoke poured from the railways,
Factory boilers and domestic grates,
Consuming coal by the hundredweights."

"Do you remember 'ow 'e'd deliver coal?
On 'is back, down the 'all to the coal-'ole.
Everytime the coalman went down the 'all
Yer gran put a little tick on the wall."

"Why was that?" I asked, unable to recall
Those symbols on the brown lincrusta wall.
"To count the number of bags emptied: I've
'eard they would drop four and say it was five!"

"Cheating? In days when doors were left open?"
"They weren't neighbours, you know. They were tradesmen.
Anyway, there was no need to conceal
Something that nobody would want to steal.

"We 'ad a wireless, and over the grate
Yer gran kept souvenirs like a blue plate
From Rhyl, and that alsation made of pot.
Before the war we didn't 'ave a lot.

"In the parlour we 'ad a three-piece suite,
But that was for them walkin' down the street
And lookin' through the window, the way they
Did. But we'd sit in there on Christmas Day.

"I can smell the cigar smoke now and see
Yer dad and my dad by the Christmas tree;
Side by side on the settee sipping beer
And saying the things they said every year."

"I can remember. It was like Sunday
Except I wasn't allowed out to play.
More family than seats, locked in that small room
With fading daylight and increasing gloom."

"Can't say I remember you complainin'."
"Cold meat for tea with pickles and gherkin
Followed by more mince-pies and marmalade.
A stomach full of wind from lemonade."

"Food was everywhere on Christmas Day,
An' in the front room yer gran'd put a tray
With a bowl of walnuts and bunch of grapes
And a packet of twenty Players Weights."

There were other treats such as sticky dates
Packed like fresh faeces in small wooden crates;
The smell of gas from the spluttering fire
And, in the background, the Bakelite choir.

"They were 'appy days, they were," Cathy sighed.
Yer gran'd get dressed up all dignified
In a black dress and she'd look a real treat
With lipstick and touch of rouge on her cheek."

"And those thick-rimmed glasses she used to wear
With matching butterfly clip in her hair;
The balls of white wool on her slippered feet,
Standing on a stool to carve the roast meat."

"Although yer gran was short, she was the boss:
When I was small, she'd take me across
'er knee. Mind, me dad 'adn't recovered
Fully from the war and 'e'd discovered

"When 'e got 'ome from that 'ospital on
German soil that 'is pre-war job 'ad gone.
The war 'ad been over two years by then
And 'e 'ad to start all over again.

"There was no work for the ex-servicemen
And no benefits like today, and when
'e came 'ome after defending this land,
They gave 'im an 'ammer, nails and shoe-stand.

"But granddad wasn't a practical man:
'e wasn't much good with tools or oilcan,
And 'is 'ands were soft. More the artist type.
That reminds me, I've got another gripe."

I had hoped she had forgotten the book,
But once again she had acquired the look
That incorporated a question-mark
Clarified by her following remark.

"Why did you write yer granddad 'ad old 'ands?"
I explained once again that different strands
Are woven to make a character whole,
And those hands are extensions of my soul.

" And it isn't proper for a grandson
To write me mam lost 'er teeth one by one.
Yer gran's teeth came out in the dentist's chair
Just like my teeth did. And d 'yer think it fair..."

Short Stories without Rhyme or Reason

THE SHOOT

The sun was as bright as burnished copper but the Welsh village was still asleep as the tousle-haired youth stood on the country lane beneath a signpost that read ' Crosville Bus Stop '. The long steel barrel of the shot-gun by his side glinted, and the boy allowed himself a small smile as he reflected on the success of the two-lined advertisement he had placed in the Farmers Weekly the previous week: RABBIT SHOOTER FOR HIRE. 6p A RABBIT.

" I don't like him having that gun, Hughie," his mother had said to Clive's father. " I don't know what you were thinking; loaning him the money."

" He'll be all right. It's better than the pistol he wanted," the father replied. " He's fifteen. Can't treat him like a child forever."

In the back garden the boy had practised shooting at empty cans, and in the kitchen he had stripped and oiled the gun, and polished the barrel till it gleamed like a new penny.

" It's now worth twice what you paid for it, Clive," his father said.

" I'll make the gun pay for itself, Dad. You'll see."

After two weeks of target practice, he felt confident enough to advertise his newly-acquired skill. It was Farmer Jones from Llanfair Talhaiarn who responded to the offer.

As Clive scrambled aboard the single-deck, navy-blue bus the driver threw up his hands. " I surrender, don't shoot." Clive laughed out loud. " Did you bring that back from the war?" the driver asked, tilting his peak cap to the back of his head.

" It's a 410!" the boy replied proudly as he sat behind the driver in the otherwise empty bus.

" Never shoot a man in the back," the driver shouted over his shoulder as the bus rattled along the lane.

" It's best to get them right between the eyes," the slim youth asserted.

" Stop. You're making me feel faint," the driver joked.

" You're okay, mister. I only shoot rabbits," Clive reassured the plump and jolly bus driver dressed in a grey serge suit.

" What's a 410?"

" A shot gun."

" With live bullets?"

" Cartridges."

" Like the old musket?"

" Sort of, except the pellets are in their containers," the young man explained, extracting a cartridge from the leather ammunition bag slung over his shoulder and holding it up. He watched the driver's eyes in the small rear-view mirror and felt satisfaction when his brown eyes widened.

" It's big enough! Is it filled with ball-bearings?" the driver asked, one eye on the road.

" Sort of. They call it shot."

" Do you shoot anything besides rabbits?"

" Rats."

" Who do you work for?"

" Meself."

" Self-employed?"

" I'm still at school."

" Where'd you get the money for a gun like that?"

" Dad. It's only a loan. I'm going to pay him back."

The bus stopped at a row of five isolated cottages.

" Good morning, Mrs Ogwen," the driver said, as the old lady clambered aboard. " Can you manage there?"

" Of course I can," the woman replied irritably, sitting on the seat across the aisle from where Clive sat. " You talk as if I'm an old woman."

" I was just worried in case you were on the beer last night," the driver replied.

" Get on with you. One bottle of stout with a hot poker is all I have. I'm not like you, Bryn Roberts."

" It never crosses me lips."

" Go on!"

" I've never had a stout in me life."

" I hope that gun isn't loaded, young man," the round woman in black shouted across the aisle.

" No, missus."

" Thank goodness for that. The bus would only have to hit a bump and we'd all be dead," she continued. " It is a shot-gun, isn't it?"

" Yes, missus."

" My late husband had a single and a double-barrel."

Although the sun had barely climbed above the cow shed, the June morning displayed the promise of a fine summer day. Clive was dressed in grey flannel trousers, a grey shirt, open at the neck, and a green and brown Fair Isle pullover. He was ready for action.

Whatever the weather, Mrs Ogwen always wore the same clothes for chapel: a straw hat, raven black with a high, round crown and a narrow brim turned up at the back so as not to disturb the iron-grey hair bun. As reflective as a beetle's back, she had cosseted the hat for more than twenty-seven years, and it was only for two hours a week that it saw the light of day. By contrast, her long black coat was as dull as a slug and its wide curling lapels added bulk to an already plump body. Her ankles, like her hands, were red and swollen. Her right, brown-spotted hand rested on a small black bible on her knee. Clive could smell her natural body odour and found it offensive.

" No Mrs Wigmore today, Mrs Ogwen?" the driver asked.

" She's not very well. Something to do with her waterworks."

" I'm sorry to hear that. Look out, here's Owen Ellis," the driver said, bringing his bus to a halt.

" Good mornin', " the farmer said, climbing the three steps into the bus. " Crikey, Bryn. We've got Bonnie and Clyde 'ere!"

The newcomer was tall and had to bend at the hip to move down the bus. Nevertheless, his grey flat cap brushed the ceiling. His navy-blue waistcoat had once been part of a three-piece suit. Now, years later, it was worn like a pullover tucked into the broad, brown belt at his waist. He wore wide canvas braces over the waistcoat for added security.

" See old Williams has got his horses and tractor out early today, Mr Ellis, " the driver called down the bus, pointing to his right.

Clive looked out of the window as Farmer Williams passed along the edge of a growing field. He was sitting on a small narrow platform above a rotating drum and beside the wooden shaft at the shire-horse's side. The lead horse, similarly blinkered, was chained but unshafted. The pasterns of both chestnuts were white. Clive made a mental note of the farmer's name.

" What you out to shoot, son?" Owen Ellis asked from the middle of the bus.

" Rabbits, sir," Clive replied courteously, aware that this man could be a potential customer.

" Where?"

" Mr Jones' farm."

" What's 'e payin?"

" Six pence a rabbit, sir."

" 'ow many can you shoot in a day?"

" As many as you want, sir."

" This all right, Mr Ellis?" the driver shouted.

" Aye, this'll do. Next Sunday, eight o'clock?"

" Here?" Clive asked.

" Aye. I'll be in one of the fields."

" Thank you, thank you," the youth murmured as the purple-cheeked man alighted with a wave.

" That's good, isn't it, lad. Doin' good business!" the driver said, waving back to Owen Ellis.

A wide dirt path swept up and around the farmhouse on the brow, stopping abruptly at a cobbled yard where a gaggle of geese stood guard. Clive retreated to the front of the house but it was impenetrable. A low, dry-stone wall surrounded the house on three sides but the bay willow bushes planted between the wall and house had been allowed to grow unchecked. It was obvious that the occupants utilised only the backdoor.

" Anybody in?" Clive shouted towards the hidden front door.

The geese had followed him from the cobbled yard and in a line they poked their heads towards the frightened youth, flapped their wings and cackled.

" Get away, " the black-bearded man shouted, gesturing towards the geese with a smouldering clay-pipe. " Are you the rabbit-catcher?" he asked, turning his attention to Clive who had been holding out his gun between himself and the unruly flock.

" Yes, sir."

" They're just after food," the farmer said, watching the geese waddle back to their own territory beside the steel milk churns outside the small dairy. " All animals are the same. Food! Food! Food! But those rabbits; they're something else. Out of control they are. If the government doesn't do something about it soon this country will go to the dogs. See those fields there. That's what I want clearing. Make sure you don't shoot no bugger now. I'm not insured for that."

" No, sir. I'll be careful."

The farmhouse was but a speck in the distance from where Clive lay on a white flat boulder. The groups of large boulders that seemed to grow out of the ground were common and the Welsh farmer simply worked around them. The rock on which Clive positioned himself offered a solid surface but more importantly camouflage. It was a fine morning for shooting: a clear blue sky and an atmosphere as sharp as a surgeon's scalpel. The rabbits were frolicking on a burrow-riddled green border inclining towards the field. Like spring lambs, they jumped in the air and chased each other in tight circles.

'They're damaging the crops. I have to do this for humanity,' Clive thought as he took careful aim at the less active rabbit in the group. Small beads of perspiration appeared on his forehead. His hands became clammy and began to shake. When he pressed his right index-finger nothing happened. He tried again but without success. At the third attempt he realised the safety-catch was still in place. With the same rabbit lined-up in his sights, he held his breath for greater accuracy – but his whole body began to shake uncontrollably and the rabbit moved in and out of view. " It's now or never, " he whispered to himself, and pulled the trigger for a fourth time. The cocked hammer hit the percussion plate with a click. There was neither explosion nor recoil.

Remaining face down with legs splayed, he reached into his ammunition bag and extracted a cartridge. Rolling onto his side, he loaded the gun and quickly resumed his original position. The rabbits were still at play but he couldn't keep his arms still. He assumed it was because of the pressure between the rock and his elbows, and rearranged himself. Resting the gun on the rock proved impossible as he couldn't see along the sights of the barrel, and anyway his arms continued to shake.

Reverting to his original position, he once again lined up the sights of his barrel and pulled the trigger. Simultaneously the rabbits stopped running and jumping. Their tails rose into the air and they disappeared down the holes in the ground.

Despite the multi-faceted nature of a shot-gun and the abundance of rabbits on the hill, he had failed to hit a single target.

It was fifteen minutes later before a lone rabbit reappeared on the green carpet. Slowly it was joined by others until the status quo was restored. Clive's next shot was rewarded: a grey rabbit fell like a stone.

By late afternoon he had another four to his tally. Leg-to-leg he strung his catch and, with the five limp rodents hanging around his neck, returned to the farm house.

The farmer's fat wife was dragging an empty milk churn out of the dairy and called: " Let 'ave a look then."

Clive walked proudly towards her, his gun under his arm with the barrel, as his father had instructed, pointing to the ground, and a grey and black fur garland reaching to his knees.

" Got five," he announced, extremely pleased with himself.

" That's a good day's work then," she said, rotating the churn over the stone doorstep.

In contrast to the hairy, academic-looking farmer, the woman was everything Clive expected of a farmer's wife: red, round and ruffled. Under a white plastic-coated pinafore the woman wore a voluminous off-white brassiere and a flowing black skirt that stopped at the top of her wellington boots. Her mousy-coloured hair was swept back from her glowing face and held by an elastic band behind her head.

" Is mister about?"

" 'ow much does 'e owe you, boyo?" she asked.

" Half-a-crown."

" 'ere then," the farmer's wife said, taking a coin from the deep pocket at the front of the apron. " 'e's out with cows."

" Where should I put them?" Clive asked.

" Don't leave 'em 'ere," she answered, putting the coin in his outstretched hand.

With his gun by his side and the rabbits around his neck, Clive sat proud on the homeward-bound bus, hoping that Billie the butcher, who lived above the shop, would open up for the five choice carcasses.

THE VERGER

The black spire of the hill-top church was silhouetted against the evening sky. The sun had gone down but its loom of pink light back-lit the old building where, for eight hundred years, the people of Shottick and nearby villages had worshipped and buried their dead.

No road passed through the ancient hamlet of scattered cottages and the church without a name.

The sole approach to Shottick was by a side-track leading from a minor road. The cottages were built in a light-grey stone and, like the similarly coloured gravestones in the churchyard, they leaned at precarious angles to one and other. The track itself stopped abruptly at the gate leading into the impoverished graveyard and the church beyond.

Although the hamlet was surrounded by thick forest, the round hill on which the church had been built stood above the treetops and, for miles around, the people of neighbouring villages were reminded daily of God and mortality. Everyone wondered who could have built such a gigantic and isolated place of worship, but nobody ever discussed matters of politics or religion.

The smallest house in the hamlet, but closest to the church, had once been the home of the longest-serving verger-cum-handyman the church had ever known. For fifty-seven years he swabbed the paved floor, polished the brass fittings, helped dig the graves and tend the graveyard. From 1820 to 1877 he scythed the grass and, where there were no flowers at the headstones, he picked wild flowers so that in summer no grave was neglected. People walked from miles away to see the display of colour, for Old Sykes, as he came to be known later in life, did not just collect flowers randomly, he selected them by colour. Despite his lack of education, he was a talented, self-taught artist. It was rumoured he could talk to rabbits and birds in their own language, and navigate the thick forest blindfolded.

Bobby Sykes was thirteen when – to his father who was the verger/

handyman in 1820 – he was apprenticed. There was no signing of indentures. It was a casual affair, for the money earned by a verger's apprentice would not have stopped him starving had he lived alone. But Bobby lived with his mother, father, and seven brothers and sisters. Not that a verger was that well-off if the money he was paid was divided by the hours he worked. It was a ten-hour day, six-and-a-half-day week and fifty-two weeks a year.

The small cottage in which Mr Sykes and his family lived was owned by the church and whoever was verger lived there rent-free. The arrangement put an obligation on the verger: " .. we live here everyday; therefore it is only fair that I work everyday," Mr Sykes told his wife whenever she complained about all the hours he was working and how it could affect his health.

Mr Sykes would have none of it. However, he was afraid of losing his job and also worried what would happen to his family if he should die. The day then, that his son, Bobby, began working alongside him came as a big relief.

It was bad fortune that before that year was out, Mr Sykes dropped dead while helping to dig a grave. It was good fortune that young Sykes, as they at first came to know him, was in his sixth month of employment and immediately appointed verger. One day he was a thirteen year old son of the verger; the next he was the verger and the sole supporter of his family.

The priest, black-frocked and under an equally black, and wide-brimmed hat, often walked through the graveyard. He was not only a man of the cloth but also a very astute observer and whenever, with billowing cloak, he swept through the church grounds, he noted Bobby's industry. Not yet fourteen, he could help dig a grave as efficiently as any man. It was not then simply out of sympathy that Bobby got the job, but for his enthusiasm for work. And, of course, he would be paid a wage lower than that his late father enjoyed.

Although Bobby was the sole source of income – and the money going into the Sykes' household was less than before – there was also one family member less. For Mrs Sykes it was still a struggle to feed the children between Monday and Thursday. On a Friday afternoon, Bobby received from the priest his weekly stipend and until Sunday afternoon they all ate meat and vegetables. Then for four days they subsisted on bread and potatoes. And throughout the year, Mrs Sykes searched the surrounding forests for mushrooms and around the hidden lake for duck eggs.

It seemed that life would go on forever like that, but as the children grew out of school they had to go away in search of work. And then one day, Bobby had to open up the grave in which he had buried his father. He cried when he reached the coffin but cried even more when he had to cover his mother's coffin with soil.

Bobby lived alone in the small cottage that not many years earlier had been filled with noisy, argumentative children. Then he had wanted them all to disappear; and disappear they did. When he thought back to those days, it seemed no time at all but how he wished they could all be children again. But that chapter had closed and, like his father before him, and his father's father, it was all work and no play.

Twice on a Sunday, Bobby had to prepare the church for service and after each service he had to remove the clay the worshippers carried in on their boots. It was not necessary to lock the door of the church for so God-fearing were all the villagers that the door was always left on the catch so that private prayers could be said any time of the day or night. Some summer nights, after a long busy day, Bobby would sleep on a pew and the next morning set about work without a thought for breakfast, so determined was he not to fall behind with his duties.

By the time he was thirty, he had already lived alone for ten years, and although he sometimes thought about taking a wife, he knew not where to find one. But as is the way of the world, he found one when he wasn't looking.

Wendy was a regular visitor to the church but as she was usually in the company of a smart young man he assumed they were man and wife. One Sunday morning she arrived at church alone. She carried a wicker-basket, its contents covered by a white cloth. As Bobby waited for the congregation to disperse, she approached him and introduced herself as Miss Wendy Groves and apologised for her brother's absence.

" My mother, who comes to the evening service, sends you this basket of food she has cooked. She says it is her way of thanking you for bringing so much colour to the graveyard. She seems to think you have brought it to life!"

" Can't bring it to life but there are a lot of graves with no descendants left and I don't see why they should be forgotten. That's all, Miss."

Miss Wendy Groves couldn't keep her eyes off Bobby Sykes and he couldn't keep his eyes off her. Averted eyes eventually became focused, hands touched and a year later they were going for walks along honeysuckle lanes. Nature had done its duty and they were eventually married by Bobby's employer. Wendy moved into the verger's cottage and a year later their first child, a daughter they also named Wendy, was born.

By the fourth year of their marriage, Bobby Sykes had sired four children but, like his parents before him, found it difficult to make his wages stretch from one payday to the next. Conditioned by nature and nurture, he didn't let domestic hardship stand in the way of his work duties. Indeed he became even more zealous and one day, single-handedly, dug a family grave as well as assist with two smaller holes. Child mortality was high in the middle of the nineteenth century and although the villagers anticipated a high number of child deaths, it was no less painful when they occurred. Arranging the burial of small children always upset Bobby but the accidental death of a young widow and her two children affected him deeply. He buried the family in one grave and two further, but unrelated, children in the second and third graves.

It was dark when he finished work. After putting his tools away he went into church to say a prayer for the dead.

The darkness inside the fan-vaulted building was relieved only by the light of the full moon filtering through the high and round stained-glass window above the altar. With the soft light falling across his face and the brass rail where he knelt, he was conscious of another presence. He had neither seen nor heard anybody enter the church but assumed some person had come to pray, entering the church while he was putting away his tools.

Twenty rows of varnished dark-wood benches filled most of the central area but six family prayer boxes lined the wall opposite the main entrance and behind the interconnecting pillars. With his elbows on the altar railings he prayed but couldn't concentrate because the person in the body of the church was moving about. It took him longer than it should have done. When he finished praying he stood up, turned around and stared into the darkness. He could see nothing.

" I'm going to light a candle. I hope you don't mind," he said, and waited for an acknowledgement. " Are you all right?"

Again he waited for a reply. Whoever was in the church was moving along a pew but was unwilling to speak. The light from the moon touched only the edge of the altar but it was too weak to cast any light across the seating area.

Putting a match to a candle, he carried it before him, checking the space between the benches as he walked back towards the main door. If anybody was in the church they must be in a family box, he reasoned. He was about to blow out the candle, leaving it on the table inside the door, when it occurred to him that it was probably a rabbit or a fox that had got in when the door was open. With his finger around the grip of the squat candle-stick saucer, he walked across to check the family pews. It was unnecessary for him to open the waist-high doors. Looking over the short partitions was all that was needed. They were all empty. He crawled between the long benches but he couldn't find the wild animal that he was sure was hiding.

" Wheresoever you are, you can stay till morning. Nobody's going to hurt you."

Wendy was sitting in a straight-backed chair beside the small table supporting the oil-lamp when Bobby arrived home. She didn't lift her eyes from the sock she was darning.

" It was a sad day, Wendy," he said, hanging his jacket and cap on the nail behind the front door.

The lower floor of the grey-stone cottage had two rooms: the sparsely furnished living-room and a small scullery where the family washed and Wendy laundered. The cooking was done over the fire grate built into the living-room wall. It was there that soups simmered, bath water boiled and cockroaches nested. The settle, three hard chairs and small table had been in the Sykes' family for more generations than anyone knew, and had served them well.

The small, foot-square window allowed little light to enter the room but from dusk until bedtime the brass oil-lamp filled the room with as much shadow as illumination. A candle, self-sealed in an old clear jar, provided mobile lighting when carried by the apex of the string wrapped around its ridged rim. A second candle, wax-welded to a piece of slate on the table, stood ready for an emergency should the tapering black smoke from the oil-lamp expire.

Although Wendy toiled endlessly to keep the cracks between the paving-stoned floor clear of moss, it appeared regularly, especially on the route, from the door to fireplace along which she carried the well-water.

The family of six shared the two upper rooms, sleeping on home-made mattresses and pillows stuffed with straw, feathers and, in summer, winter's woollen clothing. In winter they wore the woollen clothing in bed as well as out of doors.

Nothing in the Sykes' household was surplus. Whatever the season, it had its uses. When the last goose-club weekly instalment was paid, a goose arrived and its feathers were plucked for pillows and its fats used for cooking and medication. When the children had sore throats they were forced to drink the oily substance, and when their chests were infected, the grease was rubbed into the skin. And, of course, there was celebration, after prayers, at the dinner table. After a meal of goose, the following day's dinner was soup made from its bones augmented with borage, comfrey, wood mushroom and wild shallots. But the feast of goose was so irregular they became markers in a child's memory much the same as Christmas, and that was usually when the goose suddenly appeared hanging in the scullery.

The next morning, Bobby searched the church but could find no trace of the animal. For a further half-hour he examined the walls and floor looking for possible damage where a small animal could gain entry. There wasn't even a crack, for both he and his father before him had seen to that. They had been dedicated in their upkeep of the church and its grounds but Bobby knew from experience that nothing remains intact forever and that periodic repairs are necessary. Nevertheless, he could find nothing in need of repair.

That morning he had turned-in early for work to fulfil the two extra tasks of searching the church and going to the forest edge where the bluebells grew.

On the three uneven mounds of earth he arranged the flowers in the shape of a cross. Never before could he recall, in one day, having to bury a young woman and four children from three different families. The widow and her two small children had been discovered in the lake but the other two children had died from a mysterious ailment that had struck suddenly. Although they lived in separate hamlets, it was rumoured their sickness was surprisingly similar and that they had both died the day after complaining of headaches. The mothers of the two boys had wailed at the graveside, but nobody mourned the mother and her two children. Her husband had died the year previous while chopping down a tree.

They were not local and from their dialects it was said they were Scottish – but nobody knew for sure. As a couple they were industrious but kept to themselves. When her husband died, the widow was often heard talking to herself and repeating the words: how will we now live? Again and again she muttered the same line; not with tears but wide-eyed and fearful. Her neighbours understood her deep sorrow and anxiety for without a husband or other relatives for support she would have no income. How she and her children drowned nobody knew.

Bobby thought it unjust that any child should be denied a full life but accepted the passed-down philosophy that children who died young had been chosen by God as angels and that they would reappear as new stars in the firmament. Indeed, as he walked the short distance between church and home the previous evening, he had studied the star-filled sky and wondered.

The days immediately after a burial were always difficult for Bobby and he couldn't settle down to his work until the earth was level again and the memory clouded by the everyday demands of earning a living. He thought about the coming Sunday afternoon when he would be taking his children into the woods to collect flowers and to teach them, as his father had taught his children, about nature. It helped to take his mind off the sorrowful aspect of his work.

The church stood in the middle of the sloping graveyard that was encircled on three sides by a thick wood of conifer, alder, rowan and sycamore and fringed by a dense thicket of blackthorn in full bloom. In normal circumstances, Bobby loved the spring and, although Easter and Whitsuntide church festivities meant an even greater workload, he thrilled at the awakening of nature.

The tool store, built by the verger who preceded his father, was on the perimeter of the burial ground at the forest's edge. To the rear of the store, the blackthorn provided a natural barrier, and that same eighteenth century verger had planted a continuous row of privet hedging to the other three sides. Concealed from view, the small building provided shelter from the rain and long cold winters. It was the place where Bobby re-heated his billy-can of tea over a lighted candle. It also offered refuge for the troubled mind and Billy was troubled by the strange happenings of late. As he sat waiting for his tea to re-heat he pondered on those recent events.

The movement in the church was just one of several incidents that remained unexplained. It started the previous week when the handbell, used to call the villagers to prayer, rang while in its upturned position on the table inside the church door. Something he had never before heard and no matter how he repositioned the bell he could not get it to ring unaided. The second incident happened the following day when the flames of the three altar candles blew out. The church door was closed and he was alone at the altar. There was no draught, although sometimes, depending on direction, the wind did blow under the church door. And the same day there had been a knocking at the church door, but when he opened it nobody was about. He had not mentioned any of the four incidents to anyone lest they should think he was over-imaginative.

Bobby's hide-away had been built of the same stone that had once been part of a Roman fort that occupied the hill sixteen hundred years before. The church and most of the cottages in the hamlet had also been constructed of the same material. It was rumoured that the granite blocks had been shaped by stone-age men to build their villages of round dwelling houses. It was also common-talk that some of those stones (particularly those with quartz content) had magical properties. But then most things, according to the predominantly farming community, had mysterious powers. It was just a case of unlocking that power; but nobody ever did.

As he waited for his tea to re-heat, he watched the small field-mouse that had made its home in the store-room.

" Here you are," Bobby said, throwing a piece of bread to the flagged floor. As usual, in those circumstances, the small rodent retreated into its hole but quickly put its nose out again, eventually carrying the offering back to its den.

The storeroom was windowless and in winter the only light was from the candle. In spring and summer, additional light came from the open door. When the weather was warm he moved his stool outside. It was still too early to sit outdoors but warm enough to leave the door open.

With four small stones he had fashioned a support for his tea-can above the candle's flame, and it was while he waited for the tea to warm that the outwardly opening door suddenly slammed shut. Bobby jumped up, re-opened the door and walked around the building. He checked beyond the privet hedge but there was nobody about. Neither was there a wind that could have blown the door shut. Like those other unexplained incidents, he could not recall a previous occasion when, of its own volition, the door had closed. Not a man to dwell on such things, he drank his stewed tea and returned to work.

The sky was blue and the air as fresh as the daffodils that had just spread their yellow and white petals. It didn't help Bobby's state of mind, for all he could think of was what the deceased were missing. It was on such afternoons that the children rejoiced at the first signs of the approaching summer; but those four children, recently buried, would never again see the light of day.

For twenty-five years he had tended to church and graveyard but often wished he could find other paid work. But even if there were jobs available they wouldn't want a thirty-eight year old man with a wife and four children. He was tied to the verger's job not only by lack of opportunity but more especially by the roof over his family. And like his father before him, he worried what would happen to them should he die. It would surely be the work-house.

He had climbed wearily into bed and was in the twilight zone between thought and dream when his wife said: " Somebody's knocking on the door."

Bobby remained in the half-conscious state, too tired to climb back into reality. Wendy put her hand to his shoulder and, with a shake, brought him back to his senses.

" What is it, woman?"

" Somebody is knocking at the door. Will you go down to see who it is."

Barefooted and in a long-tailed, stripe shirt, he hurried down the cold stone steps. The knocking at the door was insistent.

" I'm coming," he shouted, but when he swung the door back nobody was there. Moonlight flooded the small front garden and there was nowhere for anybody to hide. He stepped into the narrow lane but nothing stirred.

" There was nobody there," he said, climbing back into bed.

" Of course there was," Wendy argued.

" It must have been the wind," he said.

" It wasn't the wind. The wind doesn't knock on the door like that."

Before either of them could again slip into the unconscious state they both desired, the rat-a-tat returned to the door. Bobby jumped out of bed, lifted up the window and leaned into the night. But there was nobody at the door. Each time the door was rattled it was with the same rhythm: a knock then a short interval followed by three close, racing raps. Then, after a short pause, a single knock and another short pause followed by a knock that concluded the six knocks. The sequences were identical and could only have been made by either knuckle or a stout stick. And yet as soon as Bobby had opened the window to look out, the knocking had stopped. He chose not to admit concern.

" There's got to be an explanation," he said, pulling the blanket over his head.

" Do you think it could have been a bird?" Wendy asked.

" That's what it is," Bobby replied without moving the blanket off his face.

Having spent most of his childhood exploring the surrounding forest, he always said he knew the trees as well as any man. With an enquiring mind he had never been satisfied with simply walking between the trees. He observed and examined the foliage that grew in rich abundance and, with the knowledge gleaned from his own father, could name every plant and creature that inhabited the forest roof and the thick undergrowth. And now it was his turn to impart his knowledge to his own children.

Soon after Sunday lunch his four young children had led him out of the cottage towards the woodland that encircled the hill. They didn't realise it but their father was as eager to walk under the canopy of interweaving leaves as they were.

" That there is lichen," he said, pointing to yellow patterns on the rocks littering the open hillside. " They call it map lichen because it looks like a map. Those wiggly lines are like boundaries separating the different families. They're all very respectful of the other's territory."

" What is it, dad?" the eldest boy asked.

" It's a moss, I suppose. It grows like the grass. There are different types of lichen. There are orange ones and black ones."

" And yellow ones," his youngest daughter reminded him.

" I'd forgotten about that," he said, encouraging his children to ask questions.

" How can anything grow on rock?" the second boy asked.

" It's a mystery all right, but there it is right before our eyes. We can't argue with what is plain to see."

" Yes, but Carl asked how does it grow on the rock," his eldest daughter interjected, not satisfied that her father had answered the question.

Bobby studied the question before replying. Not wanting to appear ignorant before his children he hazarded a guess: " I do believe they all have very tiny — tinier than the point on a pin — suctions that holds each grain to the smooth rock."

" That's a funny flower, dad," the youngest girl asked, gently touching the white tuft of fluffy hair on a long green stalk.

" It's cotton-grass," he explained.

" Like the cotton in my dress?" she asked.

" A cousin of the plant from which cotton is made, I wouldn't be surprised."

" Did this frock grow on a flower?" the same girl continued.

" Somebody had to make it," he laughed.

" Me mother!"

" She did indeed. The cotton grows something like that plant but then it has to be made into thread."

" What's a thread?" she asked.

" Everyone knows what thread is," the eldest boy said.

" It's cotton thread like your mother uses to sew the holes you make in your clothes," Bobby explained, and satisfied they followed the thin footpath into the ancient wood.

The trees that skirted the rear of the church grew at the highest elevation on the hillside and it was a descending pathway that they followed in the half-light. Larch and pine conifers dominated the upper reaches of the forest and soon the track disappeared under a thick carpet of brown needles. Bobby didn't need a footpath to guide him to what he always referred to as the secret lake. The spacing of the trees and their species were his guide-posts.

In parts, the terrain was steep and dead trees, that had grown on thin, sloping soil unable to hold their own ultimate weight, had fallen to the ground, impeded their descent. Those obstacles were further complicated by numerous streams that flowed out of fissures in the ground and meandered down and around the undergrowth towards the wide lake in the valley below.

The deciduous trees were once again covered in young greening leaves that were slowly filling the canopies that breathed daylight between the eternal night where conifers grew tall and tight. Pale and translucent leaves allowed the sunlight to filter down to the forest floor where it painted bright patterns on the brown earth.

As they climbed down the angled woodland, the rowan and mountain ash gave way to the chestnut, and eventually oak trees and sycamore dominated the landscape.

On three sides of the lake, the long yellow branches of weeping-willow trees trailed in the water but to the south a stretch of grassland separated the still waters from the forest's edge. As Bobby and his four children emerged from between the trees, a tawny buzzard, resting on a low branch, took fright and crashing through upper branches soared up and out of sight.

Isolated and visited infrequently by the sparse populations of hillside and valley villages, the area had become an oasis for the wildlife that crept out of the forest or soared up from the valley. The lake, spring fed, teemed with aquatic life but the grey curlew plodding along the water's edge probed, with its long beak, the mud bank for worm. Overhead, and on the thermal currents generated by hill, forest and lake, a pair of ravens, black silhouettes against the pale-blue sky, rolled playfully.

An island in the middle of the lake was connected to the grassy bank by a long narrow causeway. On the island the roofless remains of a long abandoned monastery spilled into the water and a sycamore tree grew within its decaying walls. As a child, Bobby had spent many hours playing in the ruin but then the walls had been higher and the roof joists intact. In the intervening years all the wood and many stones had been removed and, indeed, Bobby's own father had taken a piece of timber to make a mantleshelf over the cottage fireplace.

Instructing his children to keep in a line away from the water's edge, they walked across the causeway. It was merely the object of the exercise, the conclusion of a journey. Apart from the wildlife, there was little to see other than a demonstration of how nature soon reclaims the land. However, the mounds of stones exposed to the sun provided an excellent place to sit and eat the bread and cheese Wendy had packed.

While enjoying their afternoon meal, they watched the pair of mallards swimming in circles. The sunlight glinted off the unreal green, glassy head of the male duck while the more sombre-coated female trailed in its wake. On a nearby stone, a robin perched, waiting patiently for a crumb of bread while, high in the sycamore tree, a willow warbler sang its repetitive song. But the verger's cottage garden where they lived had its own wealth of birds and insects. For the children who lived on the edge of the forest they were part of everyday life. It was the lake and marine life that fascinated: scores of frogs moved towards their mating season among the reed at the margins of the lake where sticklebacks and newts flourished in the shallow waters. Resting vertically with their gossamer, glossy wings outstretched, dragonflies and the smaller and more delicate red damselflies sucked at the robust stalks of the common reed.

It was a beautiful day but Bobby could not dismiss the thought of the tragedy that had unfolded some weeks previous in those very waters. One of the children must have fallen off the causeway and the mother and the second child must have also perished in a rescue attempt, he told himself. Whatever the facts of the matter, that was the explanation he wanted to believe.

" Shall we head back home?" he asked his children.

" Can we catch a fish first, dad?" the eldest boy asked.

" Nothing to catch with," he replied. " We've got a lot of uphill walking from here. This is the hard part, you may recall."

And so Bobby and his four young children began the long and arduous hike up the ascending forest. As instructed, unnecessarily by his wife, he had kept the children away from the edge of the water but allowed them, in pairs and holding his hands, to watch the fish and sparkling dragonflies.

The sky had clouded over and it was the underlying and rain-bearing cumulus cloud approaching fast from the west that prompted Bobby to make a move. When they had left home early in the afternoon there had not been a cloud in the sky and the pine-cone on the window ledge of the cottage had been open wide.

As the cloud mass rolled overhead, the forest darkened but there was just sufficient light for Bobby to lead his children through the dense undergrowth. When the rain came, it drummed insistently on the canopy of leaf and leaked into the forest until Bobby and his children felt they were swimming in a green bog. Translucent and verdant, the half-light threw deep shadows between the crowded trees and seemed, crab-like, to crawl over the moss-laden boulders and up ivy wrapped tree-trunks.

In the massive root-pad of a fallen pine tree, Bobby, with his hands, dug away the soil from between the lower roots and made a shelter big enough to keep them all out of the rain. He prayed the rain wouldn't last: he had to prepare the church for the evening service and, in the dark, it would be difficult with four children to journey through the forest. The interconnecting leaves of the trees had kept off the full force of the rain but nevertheless their clothes were wet. He had never missed a day's work in all the years since he was apprenticed to his father. But that was the lesser of his concerns. His primary concern was for the health of his children: he knew that spring nights could be fatally cold for children dressed in wet clothing and without any cover from the elements.

" I think we've got to keep going, children," Bobby suggested, but simultaneously the forest was lit by lightning and followed immediately by a clap of thunder. The children pressed against each other. " But we'll have to wait till that passes."

The interval between the second flash and subsequent thunder-clap was wider than the first one, and the third combination even greater. With the passing of the thunder-storm, the air grew cooler and some of the darkness lifted. The rain stopped, and father and children hurried homeward. In the diffused forest light nothing moved in the aftermath of the tempest except the sporadic raindrops hitting the ground. It seemed all the wildlife had sensibly gone to ground.

It was a great relief to the father when he saw the faint track leading out of the forest.

After a meal, a standing bath in a bucket and goose-grease rubbed on their chests and backs, the four weary children were put to bed. Had the sun been shining, the early evening call of the outdoor may not have been strong enough, for they were truly exhausted. Bobby got to the church in good time and the evening was uneventful.

During the night the children were restless, calling out in their sleep and towards dawn they all began coughing. By morning they were perspiring and too weak to climb out of bed.

Wendy heated the remaining grease and applied it to the children's chests. With the blankets from her own bed she covered the children in an attempt to sweat the fever out of them.

" I'll have a word with the priest. He'll know what's best," Bobby said, putting on his jacket for work.

It was mid-morning before the priest arrived at the church. Bobby excused himself before explaining the nature of his children's sickness, and the priest agreed to call at the cottage to say a prayer.

The freshness that followed the previous day's storm had been replaced with a depression under a bland white sky. Although a religious man, Bobby knew that prayer alone was not enough to repair sickness. If they were no better by midday he would, he decided, during his meal break run down to the lower village and call on the doctor.

During the first part of the morning he had cleaned the church floor, polished the brasses and replaced the candles on the altar. There had been no notice of any burials that week and that factor would lessen his workload.

It was after conversation with the priest that he walked across to the tool-room on the edge of the graveyard. The door was open. He always closed the door after work but reasoned it must have been off the catch and blown open by the storm.

With one foot in the door he stopped, frozen by the sight of what stood before him: dripping water, a woman and two children stared unblinkingly.

He thought he recognised the woman but asked: " Who are you?"

There was sadness in the woman's face but bewilderment in the expressions of the young boy and girl. They remained silent, and for the first time in his life, Bobby felt helpless and afraid. Standing before him were the mother and her two children who he had lowered into the hole he had dug, and whose coffins he had covered with earth. He put a hand to his forehead but even in his disorientated state still registered that his skin was cold and damp. He turned instinctively: two other children, as though sculpted from marble, stood side-by-side with their backs to the privet hedge. He ran past them, short-cutting through gravestones. The three recent graves were still sealed by the earth that had begun to level out. He ran into the church but the priest had gone. He hurried to the altar and without reason lit a candle. Confused, he knelt to pray but didn't know what thoughts to convey. He hurried out of the church and ran back to the tool-room. The children who had stood outside the small building had gone. He hesitated on the doorstep, fearful, confused and in a state of shock he had never before experienced. With blind will-power he drove himself through the open door. It was exactly as he had left it the previous day. Nothing was out of place and the woman and children he had seen minutes earlier were no more.

Shaking from the unnatural experience, he returned, with spade and pitchfork over his shoulder, to his duties. His first task was to ensure the earth above the three recent graves was compact. Although a visual inspection was enough, he sought further reassurance by prodding the clay lumps with the pitchfork. Thoughts that made no sense raced through his mind and he found it impossible to carry on working. Underpinning the confusion was an urgency to return home.

" The priest was here about half-an-hour ago. He said a prayer,"

Wendy said.

" How are the children?" Bobby asked, climbing the stairs.

" Just the same."

The two girls and two boys, paired to each bed, lay bathed in perspiration but shivering.

" I'm going for the doctor," Bobby said.

" But do we need to now the priest has said a prayer?" Wendy asked.

" They need medicine, not prayers," her husband replied, pragmatic from his years of close-proximity with the results of reliance on prayer alone.

" Can we afford a doctor?" she asked.

Bobby ignored the question and soon after midday returned with the doctor in the doctor's horse and trap.

Within a day the fevers had subsided and by the second day, after the doctor's visit and medication, the four children were eating gruel for breakfast and broth for lunch. Wendy was back in her domestic routine but Bobby was not fully recovered from his ghostly experience. He was not a man prone to exaggeration or imagination. He was a practical man with more than a fair share of common sense. If any man were to talk of having seen a ghost, it would not be expected to come from Bobby's lips. The problem was he couldn't stop thinking about what he thought he had seen. But he told nobody, and said a thanksgiving prayer for his children's recovery.

The blossom fell from the trees and the pastels of spring turned vibrant. By late June the hillside was iridescent and skylarks, unseen on the wing, filled the air with song. It was the verger's favourite month, for the days were long and it was usually warm and dry. It was a period of renewal, but people still died and the ground could be rockhard. It took the diggers twice as long to dig a grave in summer but then fewer people died during those few months than in the long, harsh months of winter that sometimes seemed never-ending.

As though in gratitude to the Almighty, Bobby worked even harder and at the altar the brass rails and candlesticks gleamed, the church floor and ledges were spotless and the graveyard a mass of flowers. The parishioners were full of praise - but it was usually the priest, who did nothing more physical than exercise the soul, who received the accolades. Not that Bobby minded: attributes direct to a man who sought nothing more than self-satisfaction would be meaningless. The priest, with half-a-mind on metaphysical heaven, welcomed adulation; and the verger knew that as long as the praise continued, and he had his health and energies, his job and tied-cottage were secure.

Although it didn't affect his work, since the spring, Bobby had been plagued by dreams so real and disturbing that he thought of them as nightmares. The theme was repetitive but he only realised that when he entered a dream. In the morning he was unable to reconstruct fully what had passed through his sleeping imagination. Somewhere within every dream there was the image of the drowned mother and two children by the lake. And every morning when he awoke he had a strange compulsion to visit the lake.

The verger's work was lonely but he hadn't taken on an apprentice as he hoped one of his sons would one day work alongside him. As he toiled in the church and its surrounding grounds his thoughts returned often to the images that had, that spring day, presented themselves in and around his store-room. He tried repeatedly to analyse what caused such vivid imagery. He had no doubt he had hallucinated and could only put it down to the soaking he had experienced that previous day. The same soaking that had brought on his children's fever. And he was convinced the spectre was responsible for the dream that replicated itself each night.

All of those incidents that had occurred within a few days of the apparition were explainable: an animal in the church, a bird pecking the cottage door, and wind-driven doors. It was easy to dismiss the unseen but he couldn't dismiss what he had apparently seen with his own eyes; imaginary or not. He could no longer enter the store without trepidation and when he did enter he felt a chill. Whatever the weather, the temperature in the store-room remained cool. It hadn't always been that way and he considered asking the priest to exorcise the room. It was a line of thought he didn't pursue: the priest may question his sanity. To suggest that any part of a church was haunted by the dead was tantamount to sacrilege. He sought out an explanation for the low temperature and found one: the hedge surrounding the store had grown to a height that, except within an hour each side of midday, blocked out the sun.

On the last Sunday of June he awoke from a sleep tormented by images of the dead. For once the nightmare had not fragmented under the weight of consciousness but remained intact. The dream had led him down to the lake where the young woman and her two children picnicked on the island. And as usual there was a black image. It seemed to float in the air like a raven or a large crow.

That afternoon, after the morning shift, was his to do what he wished: Wendy had taken the children to her mother's house in the lower village and wouldn't be returning until early evening.

The sun was at its zenith when, with bread and cheese in his pocket, he began his journey through the thick, dark forest. Unencumbered, he jumped streams and fallen trunks, slithered down steep, thick carpets of brown pine-needles and climbed through chest-high bracken. The forest was at its formidable best and its translucent canopy unified the multifarious yellows and greens.

Emerging from the forest, it was a natural reaction to breathe deeply and Bobby held his head to the sky. In the twenty-fives years since he was a boy, the forest had grown stronger and he had to admit it had become more difficult to navigate.

With his eyes closed, he allowed the sun to warm his face – but for too long he held his head back. When he opened his eyes his vision was momentarily impaired and the woman on the island was duplicated. There were many people on the island but as his sight returned to normal it became clear that there was only one woman with two children. They were chasing something. It looked like a butterfly but because of the distance he couldn't be sure. And then a figure dressed all in black came from behind the stone wall where the sycamore grew freely. With a leap, the cloaked figure embraced the woman, forcing her to the ground. The two small children ran to their mother's defence but she gestured wildly for them to run away. They ran towards the causeway but then returned and jumped on the back of the figure lying on top of their mother. As the figure half-turned to dislodge the children, the woman picked up a stone and brought it down on the head of her assailant. At the same time one of her children pulled away the cowl. It was the priest. The woman put her teeth to the hand that restrained her and as the injured man withdrew his hand, his ring came off his bleeding finger.

Freed of the man who had pinned her to the ground, and with her two children holding her hands, she ran silently towards the causeway but, in her panic, she didn't see the large stone at the lake's edge. It was the speed at which she was running that propelled her and her two children through the air and into cold water.

As Bobby ran towards the causeway, the priest walked to where the mother and children stood in the shallows. The priest stood above them and, still holding her children's hands, the mother moved backwards, away from the bank.

" Stay there. I'm coming," Bobby shouted, but they all ignored him.

Suddenly mother and children stepped off the shelving and disappeared into deeper water.

Bobby dived into the waters he knew well: it was there that as a child he had learned to swim. Clear and unpolluted, he should have had no difficulty in finding them for he had entered the water almost immediately they went under and in the exact same place. And yet there was no sign of them. As his head broke the surface he looked for the priest but he too had vanished. But how could the priest be on the island, Bobby thought, when he had left him in the church.

Everything he had just witnessed made no sense. He had recognised the woman and her two children. He had met the woman the day he had buried her husband. They were the same people who had appeared in the church store-building. Again he swam beneath the water but it was instinct and not logic that drove him below the surface for a second time. There was nobdy on the lake bed and no current to carry away a body; but he didn't expect to find anybody.

Despite the growing realisation that it was his mind that was playing tricks on him, he nevertheless searched the small island. He was alone without even the company of the resident birds. The sun was still high and the heat caused the ground and lake to shimmer.

" I must have sunstroke," he said to himself, choosing to sit on a stone where the imaginary re-enactment had taken place.

Removing his jacket and shirt he spread them on the ground to dry. The fabric-wrapped bread was soggy but the cheese was still edible. Attracted by the food, a robin sat on a nearby rock.

" There you are, Red Robin," he said, throwing a piece of wet bread. " You must think I'm going mad, diving in the lake fully clothed."

Sitting in the sun reminded him of those childhood days when he had swam naked in that same lake, swung from the tree and fought imaginary battles on the ruined building.

" It's my imagination, Robin. It's playing up in me old age," he said, throwing another piece of bread to the bird. " I'd better cover me head before I go completely mad."

It was when he picked up the small piece of wet fabric to place on his head that he saw metal glinting from a cleft in a jagged granite rock. With the aid of a twig off the tree, he recovered a ring. He recognized it as the ring the priest had said he had lost when he injured his hand. He didn't say how or where he injured his hand but Bobby remembered distinctly that it was shortly before they found the three bodies in the lake. For half-a-day Bobby had searched for the ring in the church and graveyard but, of course, he now realised he would never have found it. He was searching the wrong place.

Only divine intervention, he reasoned, could have guided his dreams and brought him to the exact spot where the missing ring lay hidden. But that couldn't explain what he thought he had seen. It didn't mean the priest had attacked the woman and been the indirect cause of the death of the woman and her children. If what he had seen was a true enactment, then it may be said the priest was guilty of murder. He dismissed the thoughts as nonsense and, although his shirt and jacket were not fully dry, he dressed and, with the ring in his pocket, began to walk across the causeway.

He was perhaps half-way across when something caused him to turn. There, between himself and the island, the woman and her children, bowed and bedraggled, stood holding hands. Bobby closed his eyes and rubbed his eyelids; but when he re-opened his eyes, the family was gone. He resumed his journey but as he reached the pasture to the south of the lake he caught sight of the black-cloaked figure running into the forest.

" Stop," he shouted, running close behind the tall, hooded man and into the forest.

Like the mother and children on the causeway, the figure suddenly disappeared. Bobby stopped, looking in all directions through the tree spacings. Nothing moved and only silence prevailed. If somebody was running through the trees, the sound of breaking branches could not be concealed. Bobby realised his eyes were still seeing things that were not really there. But the piece of black cloth caught on a shoulder-high branch was not imaginary. He recognized that too as the piece of fabric the priest had said had been torn from his cloak in the churchyard. The fleeing figure in the black cloak had led him straight to the missing piece of fabric. And Bobby recalled that the cloak had been torn about the same time as the ring went missing. He remembered thinking how strange for a man of God to suffer two misfortunes so close together. He pocketed the torn fabric with the ring. By the time he reached the village, his shirt and jacket had dried but become re-soaked with perspiration.

As he walked down the lane he was met by the scene that never failed to make his heart miss a beat: Wendy sitting on the doorstep with her long, brown skirt tight around her ankles and the children playing in the garden. With his back to the wall, he sat on the ground beside her and held her hand.

It was after the children had gone to bed and as Wendy sat darning in the low light from the oil-lamp that Bobby, after much soul searching, said: " I want you to listen carefully to what I have to say and then tell me if I'm going mad."

" If anyone's going mad it's me; looking after those children all day. Go on, get it off your chest..."

In a low voice he began by explaining the strange happenings, but Wendy interjected immediately.

" I knew it was the devil knocking at our door," she began, but Bobby corrected her assumption.

" I think it was the dead seeking our help."

" The dead!" Wendy exclaimed in alarm.

" Keep your voice down. You'll wake the children."

Religion encompassed all aspects of life but nowhere, in the mid-nineteenth century, was it more embracing than in those rural villages with their own churches. The church was the heart of village life and its priest the brain. Wendy was aghast at the very suggestion that the person most respected in their community could be implicated in a crime of violence.

" I think you've been working with the dead for so long that you're thinking like them. I've never heard so mush foolishness in all my life. Have you been in the Coach and Horses?"

" Of course I haven't, woman," Bobby replied, regretful for having allowed his wife into his private thoughts. He considered retracting the statement but the same compulsion that forced him to visit the lake drove him on. " Please listen to all I have to say, and show you, then have your say. But please do not draw a conclusion from half a story."

" Aye, and a story it is too," she said, but, in the face of his resignation, apologised.

Bobby continued to relate the strange happenings but Wendy wasn't distracted from her needlework. It was when he related the apparition at the out-building that she stopped darning. While she could not accept the priest was guilty of a crime, she did believe in ghosts. After all, it was common knowledge in and around Shottick that the spirit lived on but could not rest in peace until torment was resolved. In those circumstances it was not unnatural for the spirit to manifest itself – but usually seen only by family. Ghost-sighting was the main topic of conversation around the tavern fire late on a winter's night and nearly every old villager could recall seeing one. Wendy's curiosity was morbid and she wanted to know every detail of how the ghostly visitors had looked and what they had said. When Bobby replied they had said nothing, disappointment registered on her face.

The darning was forgotten and Wendy sat on the edge of her chair urging Bobby, when he paused for thought, to get on with it. Listening to the first-hand experience of a spectral encounter lowered Wendy's temperature and her breathing became shallow and hurried.

" Are you all right?" he asked, concerned that his story was affecting her nerves.

" Yes, of course. Go on, what happened next?"

At the end of the tale, and after Bobby had produced the ring and torn fabric, Wendy was confused: she believed the ghost story but could not accept that a priest would do such a thing.

" What should I do?" he asked.

" Nothing. Get rid of that ring and piece of cloth. Goodness, he might think you stole his ring! Have you thought about that?"

" I hadn't thought of that," Bobby admitted.

" If the priest gets wind that you've been muck-spreading, you'll be out of a job and we'll lose our home."

As his wife insisted, he said nothing and, without any real evidence of the priest's involvement in the death of the woman and her children, continued to work for the man and church. As his wife reminded him continually, jobs were few and far between.

For thirty-two years the apparition visited him every spring. Only the frequency of the spectre was consistent: the ghosts of mother and two children appeared in the churchyard, the forest or in his dreams – but they were not ordinary dreams; they were as realistic as life itself and lasted for a whole night.

It was after one such nightmare, and on the Monday of his seventieth birthday, that Bobby found the priest hanging from the chestnut tree on the edge of the graveyard. Nobody could explain how the frail, eighty year-old priest, cloaked and hooded, could have climbed to such a high branch.

Before the next Sunday service, the synod had appointed a replacement priest, and the new priest was happy for Bobby to continue working – but as an assistant to the young man he had brought from his previous parish. The tied-cottage, however, would be transferred to the new verger, and Bobby and his wife would need to find somewhere else to live.

" Do you have any children living in the village?" the priest enquired.

" A daughter but she has a cottage full of children. My other three children are living in London," Bobby explained.

" Not to worry. We've got a week to sort it out. Come on then, let's get back to work."

Bobby walked away. The life of digging and cleaning had left its mark and his once straight back had rounded. He knew he could no longer work with the energy and pace that he possessed even a few years earlier. The ghostly visitations had filled his conscience with despair and slowly stripped his enthusiasm for life itself.

The new verger had his own ideas of how things should be done and began implementing them the very first day. There would be no picking of wild flowers for the unattended graves. " Makes the relatives lazy," he said.

The first three days after the instalment of the new priest and his verger were, to Old Sykes (as the new generation of villagers came to refer to him), very difficult. From the first day he knew he wasn't wanted and felt like a stranger. He didn't want to lose his job, for without the small wage it paid he would have nothing. There was no compassion or benefits for those who did not work.

The sky was so blue and the air so warm that it felt like mid-summer rather than spring. It was the first Saturday after the death of the old priest and the new priest had yet to conduct his first service. As Bobby pulled the weeds out of the earth at the side of the path leading to the church, he reflected on how quickly the years had passed since that first day he worked alongside his father and how proud he had been. Then, old age seemed a thousand years away. Looking back from the perspective of three score years and ten, those youthful days seemed just a few years back.

" Good morning, Sykes. Lovely day," the priest said, casting a black shadow over the kneeling assistant verger. " Don't get up. Don't want to interrupt a working man," he continued with forced laughter. " I want you to take the afternoon off. I'd like you to show my wife and children the lake. Believe there's a short cut through the forest."

" It's a long walk, sir."

" She's determined to visit the area. You know what it's like when a woman gets something into her head. Here they are now. Darling! Over here." The priest's young wife with their two children by her side walked along the path towards where the priest stood above old Bobby. " Come and meet Sykes. Hear he knows the forest like the back of his hand. He's volunteered to take you down to the lake."

With the sun at their backs, the woman and her children smiled down but, from where Bobby knelt, they were in silhouette.

" Nice to meet you, ma'am" he said.

As the newcomers turned towards the priest, the sunlight fell across their faces. Bobby felt a sharp pain deep in his chest. He began to perspire and struggle for breath. In the flesh, the dead woman and children had finally returned. He looked up to the priest for help but the family was already walking away from the church. He tried to call out, but his voice failed him.

The priest, his wife and daughter went through the gate without turning around. The boy looked back briefly at the old man lying on the ground but said nothing. And a raven pecked at the earth Bobby had loosened, flying away with a pink worm hanging from its hooked beak.

ASSERTION

" Alfred," she screamed in her grating voice, causing his back to arch and his mind to leap back four years to the day he sat with the dentist's steel drill gyrating in his mouth, " 'ow long yer goin' ter be?"

" Am coming, Virginia," he shouted meekly from the upper floor where he was tidying the bedrooms.

" And don't forget to clean under beds," she shouted, perched on the edge of the fireside chair where she pulled the black nylon stockings up over her thick, red legs. " 'e's got no gumption," she muttered to herself, as she secured the stockings with broad elastic bands that cut a permanent red ring above the knee of each mottled leg.

Alfred, with a bad dose of the flu, had been off work for a week-and-a-half, but he hadn't been lying in bed. Well, he had spent the first two days in bed, but as soon as the fever had been sweated-out of his body he had been kept fully occupied washing the dishes, sweeping and dusting, as well as preparing and cooking the meals. Without complaint, he had struggled with those domestic chores, and only very close scrutiny revealed the signs of nervous tension. Beneath a mask of resignation, he plotted and planned, but at an underlying level he was aware that placidity was his dominant emotion.

For forty-seven years, Alfred had remained a bachelor, until one day, through no particular fault of his own, he had found himself in the registry office saying, " I do". The carefully ploughed and cultivated field that had been his life was suddenly and violently turned upside-down. The shallow channels of his direction were erased and a state of flux created in his static mind. The reciting of a few words and signing of a piece of paper had turned his leisure hours away from Penningtons Tannery into drudgery. That may sound like an exaggeration. It wasn't total drudgery – he was allowed to listen to the radio while washing the dishes or polishing the brass fittings that usually hung from the wall over the fireplace and to each side of the wide, oak-panelled mirror. And he was allowed access to Virginia's extensive collection of romantic paperback novels.

Before marriage he had enjoyed his time away from the leather works – but he had never found a vestige of pleasure working in the factory. For one thing, he couldn't stand the smell, but he never bothered to look elsewhere. He knew he was comfortable in routine and, apart from Ted, the foreman, he was treated with respect. He simply went to work without thinking much about it.

You might say it was an accident – the wedding that is. A most unfortunate accident to Alfred's way of thinking...

The pollen was in the air, Alfred was living with his married sister Kate, Kate's husband wanted Alfred out of the way (not that he was any trouble, more like an old piece of shabby furniture that didn't go with the flowered decor of the semi-detached council house). Kate's husband worked with a man who had a sister married to a man with a spinster second-cousin of fifty-three who was searching for a man, any man, to be her husband – in name only: she had gone too long to spoil the circumstances of nature. And so it came to pass, by the wiles and ways of determined humanity, the two came to meet.

For six months, Virginia, as she was aptly named, had lived alone in the two-up and two-down terraced house, the only home she had ever known. The last of her parentage had expired with a distressing explosion that blasted her into the hands of a marriage bureau; but there had been no takers. Her introduction to Alfred was fortuitous.

In the blur of an uncomprehending moment, Alfred stood smiling and holding Virginia's hand. No, she was holding his, as they stood in the queue lining the oak-panelled staircase and behind a blaze of West Indian immigrants, also eagerly anticipating the joys of marriage.

" Do you take this woman to be thy lawful-wedded wife?"

Alfred didn't feel the full weight of his new burden until after the party. The reception was held in a spare room at the Salvation Army Meeting House, and Alfred was given considerable latitude in devouring buns and drinking thick tea, even talking and laughing.

The party was over by two o'clock in the afternoon and, as the pair waited outside the Union Hotel for the number twenty-six bus, Alfred suggested that a half-pint of beer might be in order, a sort of climax to the tea-party. Standing squarely on her thick, black-stockinged legs, corpulent bosom heaving from the short walk, she stared down at Alfred. He gave a little falsetto chuckle to illustrate the joke.

He'd never really smelt her odour until he sat trapped between her and the window of the number twenty-six bus. He put it down to excitement.

Virginia's little house had been furnished by her late parents fifty-five years previously, but was, with meticulous care, well preserved: wood polished, metal shining, glass gleaming. Alfred had never stepped over the doorstep before that day although, the day of making the wedding preparations, he had, inadvertently, stood on the donkey-stoned step.

" You stupid ass..... I scrubbed it this mornin'," she had cried.

On arrival home from the wedding reception, Virginia got on with her knitting and Alfred busied himself in 'Love in the Rose Garden' that she said he could read. The evening was similarly passed with the exception of the hour listening to the radio; neither really concentrating, each, for different reasons, wondering about the other. Although Alfred, from time to time, turned the pages of the book, his thoughts were in a different sphere: ' What should I do when we go upstairs? Is she expectin' me ter ask 'er up now or would she think it cheeky of me?'

And so the thoughts rotated in his head. But Virginia had no such thoughts. Alfred's bed was made – in the back bedroom. Hers was the double in the main room. She was wondering if the first day was, perhaps, too early to set him agate. 'That window cord'll be 'is first job, then the ladders need doin'... no, 'e'll 'ave ter do the ladders first so's 'e can do windows. The lavatory needs painting. He can do that on Wednesday, 'e's got three days off work; and that slate that's loose..... 'e might be a bit old for goin' up there, though 'e says 'e's only forty-seven. Fancy me a bride. What would me Mam and Dad 'ave said? Never mind, Mam and Dad, he won't touch me. Your little girl'll be safe.'

That night, at ten-fifteen to be precise, Alfred was led to his bedroom and, without further words, the two retired to their separate rooms. Double bolts rolled into place and barred the alien world from the hairnetted and uncorsetted bride. Only sound penetrated the walls and her snores echoed in Alfred's night. Before he had slipped into the fretful sleep, he tossed and turned until the rigid wire of a broken spring plunged through his new flannelette pyjamas, puncturing flesh and determining his sleeping position. Already the tide was creeping in over the sand, and the sky was growing dark.

Alfred was out of bed as soon as he heard the milkman. Not that getting up early was anything unusual for him: it had been that way all his working life and rising at seven, putting the kettle on and brewing the tea was an automatic reaction, done without any question of forethought or malice. Virginia's nasal orchestrations were still reverberating around the house when Alfred climbed into his new charcoal-grey trousers. He carefully folded the pyjamas, trying to recapture the original creases, before tiptoeing down the narrow staircase. While waiting for the water to boil he tried to assess his new position and a smile crossed his face as he considered what an adventurous person he was: ' Why, this is the third 'ouse I've lived in.'

For forty-five years Alfred had lived in a similar, but more spacious, terraced house, a home that had been ruled over by his kindly, grey-haired mother, a woman who had struggled through widow-hood with a teenage son and daughter and smothered them with love; a mother who, with open arms, invited her new son-in-law to 'shelter under the humble roof'. Then there were three: Alfred, his sister and her husband; but very soon Alfred found he was the intruder.

He recalled, while he watched the squatting kettle, that fateful Saturday morning when the little, jovial man with the red nose had followed the bulky documents from the council office and, putting his umbrella on the kitchen table, had explained that theirs was a clearance area and that, on the appropriate form, they must mark their preference of district for a council house. With her husband's guidance, Alfred's elder sister made the decision. When they moved into the new semi-detached house by the gasworks they obligingly took Alfred with them but left the old piano behind. Alfred had always longed to learn to play it but he never got around to it; anyway, only half the keys struck any chord. On the first day in the new house he had been overtaken by feelings similar to those that possessed him as he watched the craning neck of the kettle's spout: a mixture of adventure, uncertainty, confusion, perhaps even fear. He returned once to see the old family house (that had sheltered him for all those years) before demolition.

It had been a grey Saturday afternoon (as he recalled, everything that he ever did away from the norm was done on a Saturday -- all his memories of adventure were stored in the seventh-day box) as he slowly walked down the ghostly street of shattered windows and gaping doorways where the wind stirred the dust and wandered freely through empty kitchens, parlours and bedrooms of the past. He looked into naked houses where, in forty years, he had never before seen beyond the lace-curtained windows. Now they where exposed and he could see through to the crumbling lavatories in their cracked backyards. ' Old Blacky used to live there, 'aven't seen him for ages, not since his weddin' in fact; must be all of twenty years ago.' Suddenly he was standing outside it; wind rumbled in the pit of his stomach. He shivered: his old house, his only real home, empty and black, raped in every room by uncaring workmen. Jagged edges of glass leering out of the window frames. Alfred had put that flowered paper on the parlour walls himself; it had taken him three weeks in the evenings and now, it was peeling off in great chunks, and... someone had drawn rude pictures on it. He stared through misted eyes and his mind flooded back to the day he had left the house holding his mother's hand and toddled off along the pavement – his eyes followed the path – to his first day at school. He remembered the little white kitten that had been bought for his sixth birthday and how he had chased it over the sofa. He could see his mother sitting in her favourite chair knitting while his father stood tapping his pipe against the fireplace. This was the house from which he had followed the undertaker twice.

The kettle bounced on the stove and he emptied the water into the brown teapot, let it settle for a minute and then poured out two cups. He pondered, not knowing whether to call up the stairs or boldly take it up to her room; 'after all, she is my missus now.' Taking care not to spill any into the saucer, he climbed the enclosed staircase to the small landing but hesitated outside her door before knocking gently, twice.

" Yes?"

" It's, it's me.. Alfred. I've got a cuppa tea for yer."

" Leave it on the step!"

He followed the curt instruction and retreated down the twelve steps to the kitchen where he sat alone sipping tea, incapable of comprehending the situation.

The weeks went by and he struggled to understand the nature of his existence. Life's condition had always been too complex. He considered everybody was like himself: puppets on strings that were manipulated by unseen hands. He had never been fully in control of his own affairs – but neither had he before been so totally dominated. For six weeks, in good health and sickness, he carried his burden without once voicing disapproval.

" Tek yer wet shoes off in the 'ouse. Don't fiddle wi' radio. Where's yer table manners? Yer like a pig! Why I married yer ah don't know. Wash the pots. Look! Yer clumsy fool: you've knocked the 'andle off me best cup. You can 'ave a tin mug from now on. Sweep the floor, make the beds, polish the furniture, clean the windows and don't forget to disinfect the lavatory."

Her voice and instructions became an integral part of his dreams, and he often awoke from a restless sleep sitting bolt-upright in bed in a cold sweat, unsure of his whereabouts.

In the cold light of dawn, slowly and painfully, comprehension set in.

" SHAPE YERSEL', MAN!"

It was the seventh Sunday of their married state, and the morning when Virginia paid particular attention to her appearance. The visit to the cemetery was the highlight of Virginia's week, and she had to look her best.

Her stockings secured by new elastic bands and her black pleated skirt smoothed down, she stood before the mirror putting the final touches to her greying hair. She watched Alfred's reflection as he appeared at the bottom of the staircase dressed in an old flowered pinafore. He put the feather duster on the table.

" Don't put it on the table, you stupid man," she shouted, without being distracted from her task nor turning around.

Alfred uncorded the apron, putting it on the table with the duster and, with purpose in each stride, moved up behind his spouse.

Wide-eyed and immobilised by the combination of Alfred's facial expression and proximity, Virginia, for the first time in her life, was rendered speechless. She felt his hands on her wide hips and his breath on her neck.

" Get down ont' rug," he demanded, emphasising each word.

That night, Alfred slept soundly -- and in the double bed.
